FOR THE REST OF ETERNITY

Christian's Coven 5

Lynn Hagen

**EVERLASTING CLASSIC
MANLOVE**

**Siren Publishing, Inc.
www.SirenPublishing.com**

A SIREN PUBLISHING BOOK
IMPRINT: Everlasting Classic ManLove

FOR THE REST OF ETERNITY
Copyright © 2012 by Lynn Hagen

ISBN: 978-1-62241-387-4

First Printing: September 2012

Cover design by Jinger Heaston
All art and logo copyright © 2012 by Siren Publishing, Inc.

PUBLISHER
Siren Publishing, Inc.
www.SirenPublishing.com

FOR THE REST OF ETERNITY

Christian's Coven 5

LYNN HAGEN
Copyright © 2012

Chapter One

Jacob walked into The Manacle, threading his way through the crowd of dancers as he sought out the bar. The club smelled of sweaty bodies, sex, and an overdose of alcohol. The place was packed with so many bodies writhing around to the music that Jacob wasn't sure he would stay for long. He hadn't come here to party or to seek out a one-night stand. In all honestly, Jacob was there for one reason only.

Shelby.

The slim man drew him here like an invisible leash tugging at his chest. Jacob wasn't sure what it was that had him so mesmerized with the man. But whatever it was, he was there…and on the hunt.

"Can I get you a drink?"

Jacob twisted around and glanced at the bartender. The man stared at him with a smile, but for some reason, Jacob could see that there was no humor in the man's eyes. It was as if he were staring at a talking wax figure. The man was pale, tall, but built with a lean figure, and had a nicely trimmed haircut that stopped at the nape of his neck. He wasn't bad looking. If someone liked wax figures dressed in nicely pressed jeans and a silk dress shirt. The indigo color of the shirt seemed to do the man justice. He gave the wax man a nod and a slight smile. "Just a cold beer."

"Coming right up," the bartender said as he rapped his fingers on the scarred wood of the counter and then walked away. At least the man acted like every bartender Jacob had ever come across.

Jacob once again stared across the crowd, noticing that many of the dancers wore some sort of gothic getup. A lot of them looked young enough to be college students out to piss their parents off. Black lipstick, eyeliner, nail polish, and so many chains and spikes adorned their outfits, both men and women, that Jacob felt underdressed. The only thing he was wearing was a pair of faded jeans and a T-shirt. Go him.

"Here you are," the bartender said as he sat the glass bottle on the counter in front of Jacob. "You're Vaughn's friend, right?"

Jacob nodded as he grabbed the bottle. "Yeah."

"On the house," the man said before walking away.

Jacob crossed his arms over his chest loosely, holding the beer in his hand but not drinking from it. With all the medication he was currently taking, drinking alcohol wouldn't be wise. For all he knew, drinking the beer would not only lay him out flat, it would probably shove him headfirst into a coma. But he didn't want to just sit there empty-handed as he searched for the man who had grabbed his attention by the horns.

Drawing attention to himself had never been his style.

Jacob glanced to his right to see his longtime friend heading his way, a knowing smirk on his mocha-colored face. His saunter was self-assured, his eyes smiling. "You came back," Vaughn said as Jacob gave a tight nod.

"I told you I would." Jacob set the beer on the counter, happy to get rid of the prop. The cold bottle felt good in his hand since the place was packed with dancers and the humidity was starting to cling to him, but the temptation to take a drink just to cool his parched throat was too much.

It was just supposed to be a prop, after all.

The noise in the club seemed to intensify all around him as Vaughn sat on one of the stools, raising his hand to the bartender in thanks.

"Where's Connor?" Jacob asked as he searched the crowd for the man with the darkest eyes he had ever seen. Shelby had to be around here somewhere. Jacob hoped so.

Maybe he should take Vaughn's advice and leave Shelby alone. But he couldn't help but feel as though he was supposed to meet the man, supposed to talk to him. It was a strange feeling, but Jacob went with it.

He'd never experienced a tugging in his gut like the twisted rope had pulled him back to this club, and he was curious to find out what it meant.

Vaughn clucked his tongue as he sat there, looking at Jacob disapprovingly. In all the years he'd known the guy, Vaughn had never given him that sort of look. He shifted on his stool, but decided he wasn't going to back down.

Jacob didn't care what the man thought of him. He was a friend, but Jacob had to live his own life. It was way too short as it was. He had just found out two months ago that he had aplastic anemia, something rare from what the doctor had told him. So he wasn't going to waste any time.

Vaughn sighed and then rested one of his beefy arms that was littered with tattoos on the bar. "I know why you're here. I told you that going after Shelby is a bad idea, Jacob."

He had heard the warning the first time, but Vaughn needed to tell that to the rope attached to Jacob's gut.

Jacob didn't think his heart could beat any faster than when he lifted his gaze and spotted Shelby on the second floor of the club clearing a table off. He looked so damn sexy up there that Jacob almost walked away from his conversation with Vaughn. That invisible rope was tugging again. It was tugging harder the longer he stared up at Shelby. The man's black hair seemed to shine under the club lights, making his eyes stand out in contrast to his pale skin.

He heard Vaughn talking next to him, but the words weren't registering as Jacob stared up at the man who had his full interest. "I think that decision should be up to Shelby," he said as he glanced away and looked back at Vaughn's dark brown eyes.

The decision should be up to Shelby. Jacob knew for a fact Shelby was old enough to make his own decisions. If he weren't, he wouldn't be taking any interest in the man, and Vaughn would have warned him up front. No, Shelby was old enough to get into a lot of wicked things with Jacob.

Vaughn stood and shrugged. His large shoulders looked as though two small mountains were sighing. The man had an expression on his dark face that said it didn't matter one way or the other to him. "Your neck."

That it was. Jacob had never backed down before for anyone, and he wasn't going to start now. "Duly noted, my friend."

Getting up from the stool at the bar, Jacob jogged up the steps and waited for a few people to pass by before he approached Shelby from behind. He had to admit, even from the back side, the man looked good. Shelby was shorter than Jacob, by about six inches, but he could work with that.

"Hello," Jacob said as the last of the customers moved away. It was just the two of them now.

Shelby spun around, his hand over his heart as he stared wide-eyed at Jacob, his chest rising and falling quickly. "H–Hi."

Jacob slid into the booth Shelby was clearing away, trying his best to seem smaller to the man, less intimidating. He had been told that he looked rough and dangerous by quite a few people. And that was the last thing he wanted Shelby to think of him as. "Shelby, right?"

Eyes growing wide, Shelby nodded his head in quick bursts. "How did you know?"

Jacob could feel his teasing nature surfacing. And that didn't happen too often. He was usually quiet, reserved. But Shelby made Jacob feel...playful. "I have my ways," he said as he wiggled his eyebrows.

Shelby stood there staring at Jacob for what felt like forever. The man's dark eyes flickered around Jacob's face as if trying to figure him out. He finally snapped out of whatever zone he was in and cleared his throat, his pale skin coloring very nicely with pink. "I'm very busy."

Damn, Jacob wanted to eat the man up. His short black hair was combed nicely to one side, giving Shelby an intelligent look. He had a black turtleneck on, a color that seemed to complement the diminutive man's complexion, but it puzzled Jacob considering it was only early fall outside. The cold hadn't even settled in yet.

"Would you mind meeting me when your shift ends?"

Shelby looked stunned as he glanced around the second floor. Jacob didn't like the fact that the man looked trapped. He may have an intimidating appearance, but he wasn't that ugly. He ran his hands over his short-cropped hair, feeling the rejection coming like a heavy weight slowly pressing down on him.

That was too bad. They could have had a good time together.

"Okay."

It was now Jacob's turn to look stunned. The man had said yes? He hadn't seen that one coming. "What time?"

"Four," Shelby said as he glanced around the second floor once more. Jacob turned, his eyes scanning the upper floor, but didn't see anyone.

"Who are you looking for?"

Shelby swallowed as he grabbed the last empty glass and sat it in the tub that was sitting on the other side of the table. There was a large collection of dishes in the tub, plates, glasses, and used napkins. "No one."

Now why didn't he believe the man? Checking his watch, Jacob saw that he had a few hours before Shelby's shift ended. That gave him enough time to go home and take his meds, shower, and come back wearing black. He did feel somewhat out of place here in his bright green T-shirt. "I'll be back at four, Shelby."

The man nodded, as if it was more of a habit than confirmation as he stared up at Jacob. "What are we going to do?"

That was a good question. Jacob hadn't thought Shelby would agree, so he really hadn't thought past asking the man. "We could go riding."

"Riding?"

"On my bike." The man intrigued Jacob, and he wanted to find out more about him. There was just something about Shelby that pulled Jacob to the guy. That had never happened before.

Shelby shook his head as he took a step back, underlying fear evident in his beautiful dark eyes. "I can't go outside when the sun comes out."

Jacob cocked his head to the side as he thought about what Shelby had just said. That was a very strange thing to say. "Are you allergic to the sun?" He had heard of people who were, but never met anyone with that condition.

"You could say that," Shelby replied as he grabbed the tray of dirty dishes, the silverware rattling around, clanging against the glasses. "I have to go. See you at four." The man hurried away, running as if Jacob would chase him down.

As cute as the man was, he sure as shit was strange. Jacob rubbed his chin as he watched Shelby run down the steps and then behind the bar. Standing, Jacob walked over to the balcony edge, resting his hands on the railing as he looked out over the crowd.

There was definitely something very strange about not only Shelby, but The Manacle as well. Jacob wasn't sure what it was, but the feeling of being someplace forbidden washed over him, seeping inside his skin. It looked like any other gothic club that Jacob had been to, but for some reason, this particular club felt…off.

"Enjoying yourself?"

Jacob glanced to his left to see a slim and well-dressed man walk up the balcony stairs. His hair was black and hung to his shoulders, moving slightly as the man walked. His eyes bore into Jacob as if he could see into Jacob's very soul. Warning bells sounded inside his head as the stranger moved closer, studying him.

"Somewhat," Jacob answered honestly.

"I am told that you are Vaughn's friend. Is that correct?"

Jacob nodded. "I am."

The man slid his hands into the front pockets of his creased slacks, walking over to Jacob, and then turned, staring off into the crowd as Jacob had done not two seconds ago. "There are many here who can satisfy whatever thirst you are seeking to quench. Tell me what you prefer, and I will make sure it is yours. On the house. Do you prefer women or men? Young or more mature? A scene in one of the BDSM rooms?"

Jacob wasn't sure what the man was after, but he wasn't interested in any of that. He was here for one reason only, and he shuddered to think that Shelby would be offered in such a way to strangers. It also pissed him off for some reason. He didn't even know Shelby aside from his name, but the thought of the small man servicing anyone made his back molars grind.

"Thanks, but I'm good."

The man turned his head. His eyes held no animosity or any other emotion. They were just pools of darkness, like polished marbles. "Then if there is nothing here you seek, maybe it is best you leave my establishment."

"On what grounds?" Jacob asked. He had done nothing wrong. The only thing he wanted was some time with Shelby, and the man had said yes.

"Because," the man began as he moved closer, anger and rage swirling in the depths of his black eyes, the stoic expression gone, replaced by something dark and demonic. "Shelby is off-limits. He is not like the rest of the men here. Do I make myself clear, Jacob?"

Not really. Jacob was having a hard time understanding why Shelby couldn't date him. What interest did this guy have in Shelby that he was warning Jacob away? "He is of age, right?"

The man's lips thinned as his face pulled back in a mask of rage. Those eyes. Jacob couldn't help but become mesmerized by them. They were just ordinary black eyes, but…not. They were starting to creep him out. The hairs on the back of his neck tried to crawl down his spine as Jacob took a slight step backward, trying his best to put some distance between them. "That is not the reason," the man ground out.

"Prince," Shelby said quickly as he ran up the steps, panic in his eyes, "you don't understand."

Prince? Jacob looked from Shelby to the man standing in front of him, feeling as though he wasn't the one who didn't understand.

"He's my…" Shelby looked from the stranger—because Jacob refused to think of him as a prince—to Jacob, his eyes wide as his hands twisted in front of him. "*Friend,*" Shelby finished.

The stranger's head snapped back as he glanced at Shelby and then glared menacingly at Jacob, those dark eyes almost blazing. "You smell of sickness," the man spat and then took a deep breath, like he was trying to tamp down his anger. Jacob was confused as hell. "Hurt Shelby and I will torture you for all eternity, Jacob Marshall." The stranger glanced once more at Shelby, his features softening, before descending the stairs.

"I'm sorry," Shelby quickly apologized. "Did you still want to meet at four?"

Jacob could hear the fear in Shelby's question, as if Jacob would wash his hands of this mess and walk away. Any sane man would. The stranger had a lethal air about him, and strangely enough, Jacob believed the man would make good on his threat. He wasn't even sure how the guy with the scary eyes knew his last name. Not even Vaughn knew his last name. And how on earth did the man know Jacob was sick? "I'll be here at four."

Shelby placed a timid hand on Jacob's arm. He could feel a light squeeze of the fingers as Shelby's eyes turned up toward him, imploringly. "Promise you'll come back?"

Jacob sighed. Everyone was warning him away from Shelby, but the only vibe he got from the short man standing in front of him was innocence, some sort of strange yearning. Was that why so many were warning him away? "I promise."

Shelby smiled and Jacob knew he was going to do whatever the man wanted. His smile seemed to light up the dark club and give Jacob a sense of pride. Where that feeling was coming from, he wasn't sure.

"I have to get back to work. I'll meet you right here at four." Shelby hesitated, leaning in a little closer to Jacob and then inhaled, his eyes fluttering slightly before he opened them fully and nodded. "Four."

Jacob watched as Shelby ran back down the steps. He wasn't sure what he had just agreed to, but he had a feeling it was about to change his life forever. Walking down the stairs and outside the club, Jacob pulled in a lungful of crisp, autumn air. He had things to do before meeting Shelby, so he'd better get on with it if he was going to be back here on time.

Straddling his bike, Jacob drove out of The Manacle's parking lot.

* * * *

"He is your mate?" Christian asked.

Shelby nodded as he sat the napkin down and turned around. "He is."

Christian ran his hand over his chin, glancing down at Shelby as his fingers played over his jaw. Shelby was terrified that the prince would forbid him to see Jacob.

His mate looked gruff and outlawish, but Shelby could see the kindness in the man's pretty light-brown eyes. He also smelled the sickness on his mate that Christian did, but Shelby wasn't as old or as wise as the prince to know exactly what the smell was.

Christian lowered his hand, his features relaxing like he had just come to a decision. "I want you to court him here, Shelby. Until I find out more about your mate, I do not want you venturing outside these walls with him. Understood?"

Shelby felt like shouting for joy, but nodded his understanding instead. "Yes, Prince."

It wasn't like Shelby could go for that bike ride anyway. Four in the morning was too close to sunrise, and Shelby knew better than to take any chances with his safety.

Besides, everyone in the club would rat him out if he took off with Jacob. He knew they were only looking out for him, but it still sucked. Most vampires around here treated him like spun glass. Shelby was stronger than that. But no one would let him prove himself. That had been fine in the past, but now that he had found his mate, Shelby felt the need to prove he was worthy of Jacob. The man was big, thickly built, and looked rough and tough. He wouldn't want a wimpy mate.

No, Shelby was going to prove he was mate material to the handsome biker.

He just wasn't sure how he was going to go about doing that.

What did Jacob like?

What did he find fun?

What were the qualities in a man he found attractive?

Shelby wanted to growl at all the questions floating around in his head. He felt frustrated.

"You look like you're about to blow a gasket," Vincent, one of the bartenders, said to him as he leaned on the counter. "Go eat a human, it helps."

Shelby spun around, pointing his finger at Vincent. One of these days the wrong person was going to hear Vincent, and then the vampire was going to be mud. "You know you're not allowed to talk like that. If the prince hears you saying anything bad about humans, he'll be the one eating you."

Vincent had tried to take Jimmy away from Nija. Those two were mates, and it was a big no-no to interfere in mating. But what ticked the prince off was when Vincent referred to humans as blood-cows, seeing humans as nothing more than cattle. Considering the prince's mates were human before Christian converted them, Vincent had to have been insane to say such a thing. Christian gave Vincent one last chance. If Vincent so much as stepped one toe out of line, the prince was going to kill the vampire.

"I don't know what you're talking about. I didn't say anything." Vincent smirked as he went back to taking orders from customers.

Shelby ignored the vampire. He had more important things to worry about. Okay, so what did he know so far? He glanced down at his body to see his black turtleneck and grey slacks. Jacob had asked him out, so he must have liked what Shelby was wearing. God, that sucked. He was only wearing his turtleneck because he hadn't fed yet and he was cold. Was he going to have to wear one all the time now?

He also asked Shelby out when Shelby was being shy. He was only that way when he didn't know someone. Would Jacob want him to be that way all the time? Did he like shy men? Obviously, he had asked Shelby out.

Okay, so wear constrictive clothing and act shy.

Shelby groaned. There was a problem with that plan. He really wasn't that shy. Not really. He was only shy when in stressful situations and getting to know someone. Other than that, he was pretty outgoing.

He really did need to learn what kind of a mate Jacob wanted. Shelby began to worry that Jacob wouldn't like him once he got to know Shelby. There was always that possibility. Shelby growled softly as he walked upstairs to clear away the tables. Dwelling on his attributes, or lack of, was only giving him a headache. He would show Jacob who the true Shelby was and then let the man decide from there.

But that thought wasn't comforting either.

Shelby went back to work, shoving his nervousness aside as he handed menus to the new arrivals at the booths and then cleared away the dishes of those who left. He understood the concept of feeding the donors. They had to keep up their health, at least after being used for food. But sometimes he didn't understand how drunken humans could even consume anything to eat.

Shelby cleared the table and headed downstairs to see Dante walking into the club, Taras at his side. Shelby gasped, wondering what that vile vampire was doing here. If he never saw that man again, it would be too soon. Taras had taken liberties with Shelby that weren't consensual. The man had tricked him into one of the BDSM rooms and tried to tie Shelby down. Thankfully he had gotten away.

Shelby stormed behind the bar, going in through the door on the back wall and into the kitchen area. He didn't want to see Taras or hear his pompous speeches. Christian had made Shelby give Taras his punishment for trying to force Shelby, and he knew Taras was still angry about being left out in the sun to burn.

Well, the man shouldn't have forced himself on Shelby.

"Why are you hiding in here, young one?" Rajharm, the cook, asked.

"Taras is here," Shelby confessed.

Rajharm hissed, tossing his tongs down and heading toward the door. Shelby quickly stopped him by running in front of the vampire and placing his hands on the man's chest. "Please don't start any more trouble. Hopefully Dante won't be here long, and he'll take Taras with him."

The man didn't look too happy, but he gave Shelby a tight nod. Shelby could see Rajharm's jaw clenching as he stared at the door. "Stay in here, Shelby."

Shelby took a seat on one of the stools in the kitchen and sighed. He knew he couldn't hide in here for long. He had work to do, but the thought of going out there and facing Taras made his stomach hurt.

"You have customers upstairs," Winston shouted into the kitchen.

Shelby stood, taking a deep breath before stepping outside. He could see the hard glare on Rajharm's face, but there was little Shelby could do. The prince had assigned him the task of feeding and cleaning up after the humans, and Shelby wasn't going to let the prince down.

He didn't see Taras, or Dante, so Shelby headed back upstairs to greet the drunken humans, who were smiling and laughing, having a good time and oblivious to their true surroundings. What would it be like to be unaware of the dark world around him? Shelby liked being a vampire, liked the world he lived in. He just hated people like Taras.

There was always a bad seed in every race. And Taras was theirs—in Shelby's eyes at least. The man didn't seem to have a kind bone in his body.

Shelby took the humans' orders and then hurried to the steps to hand in the ticket to the cook when he spotted Taras coming up the steps, alone. Shelby swallowed hard but refused to run. He didn't want Taras to know how truly afraid of the man Shelby was. Besides, Taras had already seen him. He would know if Shelby ran.

And if Shelby was going to be Jacob's mate, he had to be tougher than a whimpering puppy.

"I see you still run behind the humans and clean up after them," Taras sneered as he raked Shelby with his eyes.

"What do you want, Taras?" Shelby fought to keep a hard edge to his voice. He couldn't show any fear, although Taras probably smelled it on him.

"To let you know that I haven't forgotten your little punishment you doled out to me." Taras leaned in closer and Shelby gagged. The man smelled like fresh blood, only it wasn't an alluring scent, being on Taras's lips and all. "I will have my day, Shelby. You'll slip up, and I'll be there to get my revenge."

"Taras!"

Shelby heard Dante's harsh bark at Taras, but felt like he was going to faint right there on the steps. Taras was a very bad man, and Shelby hated him. It was vampires like Taras that gave their race a bad name.

And Shelby knew Taras would make good on his promise. The man was evil enough to do just that, which only made Shelby fear for Jacob. The man was human, sickly. There was no way he was going to get Jacob caught up in all of this.

As badly as the thought pulled at every single nerve ending in his body, Shelby was going to have to refuse Jacob and send him away. He couldn't risk Jacob getting hurt.

With a hurting heart, Shelby walked down the steps and into the kitchen once again.

Chapter Two

Jacob looked at his watch as he parked his bike in the parking lot of The Manacle. He had ten minutes until Shelby's shift was over. He wasn't sure what they would do after Shelby clocked out, but Jacob didn't really mind. He just liked talking with the man.

He nodded at the bouncer at the door who let him walk right in. The crowd had thinned, but there were people still milling around, as if leaving this place was the last thing they wanted to do. The dance floor was empty, and the music, thankfully, was no longer thrumming through the place.

Jacob glanced around, looking for the man who seemed to call to him. There was just something about Shelby and Jacob wanted to peel back the layers until he found the true core of who the man was.

Did he really just think that?

Shaking his head, Jacob knew he was losing his mind. Never before had anyone gotten under his skin like this. Jacob smiled and then chuckled to himself. He could see now that Shelby was going to be his downfall.

He spotted Shelby coming out of a door behind the bar, wiping his forehead as if he were tired from working all night.

Jacob crossed the room, meeting Shelby at the end of the bar. "Ready?"

Shelby started as if Jacob had just scared him. He reached out and placed his hand on Shelby's shoulder, his brows pulled together. "Is everything all right?"

Shelby pulled back enough for Jacob's hand to fall from his shoulder as he rubbed the back of his neck. Shelby wouldn't even look up at him. "I don't think this is such a good idea, Jacob."

"What?" Jacob asked as he felt the hairs on his arms rise. Something wasn't right. Shelby had readily agreed to meet with him. Why was he changing his mind now? Did that prince guy talk Shelby out of seeing Jacob?

"We're just…" Shelby trailed off as he bit his lip, glancing around the club. There were people cleaning up, and wiping down, no one paying them any attention. "We're just two very different kinds of people. I don't think it would be wise to intermingle."

Intermingle? "You agreed to go out with me, Shelby. I know you can't go out in the sun from whatever skin condition you have, but I don't see a problem with us hanging out here for an hour or two." That should give Jacob some time to get to know the man.

"I—you." Shelby glanced back down at his hands. "It can't happen."

Jacob was becoming extremely frustrated. Shelby called to a part of him that Jacob didn't fully understand, but he wanted to. "What can't happen, Shelby?"

"Us," Shelby said as he glanced up at Jacob. "We can't happen."

"Was it the prince?" The man was intimidating as hell. Jacob wasn't too proud to admit that, but he wasn't going to have the man bad-talking him, and the *prince* didn't even know him. Jacob may not look like much on the outside, but he wasn't a bad man.

"No," Shelby quickly answered as he shook his head, his eyes wide. "He said it was okay."

Who the hell was this guy that Shelby had to get permission from him? "Then what's the problem?" Jacob asked as he pulled Shelby's hands into his. The small contact sent pinpoints of thrill all through Jacob's body. Just touching the man excited him.

Shelby stood there staring at their hands before he glanced back up at Jacob. "You have to go," Shelby said as he pulled his hands free and backed away. "This can't work."

Jacob felt a growl rumbling in his throat. Shelby changed his mind for a reason, and he was going to find out what that reason was. "I'll go, Shelby, but I will be back. I'm not giving up on you."

"Please, you have to," Shelby whispered before he took off.

Jacob sighed as he turned and walked away. He didn't care what Shelby said. Someone had changed the man's mind for him, and Jacob was going to find out who that person was.

* * * *

Jacob found himself parking his bike in the same exact spot as the night before. He wasn't sure why he was fighting so hard to get a date with Shelby. But it didn't set right with him to just walk away. Shelby was an enigma that Jacob was going to figure out.

He walked past the bouncer, but this time he noticed the man giving him a hard glare. What the hell was that all about? Jacob ignored the man as he walked over to the bar. Taking a seat, Jacob looked up toward the second-floor balcony. He didn't see Shelby up there. Maybe he was behind the door that was behind the bar.

Jacob was going to sit here and wait. Sooner or later he was going to see Shelby, and when he did…Jacob wasn't sure what he was going to do, but sitting on his ass doing nothing wasn't the answer.

"He doesn't want to see you."

Jacob turned to see Vaughn standing behind him, his arms over his chest. "And once again, that's a decision for Shelby to decide."

Vaughn sighed as he lowered his arms. "Look, Tiny. We're good friends. So that's why I'm telling you now to back off. You have no idea the protection Shelby has all around him. It isn't wise to stir the pot. Trust me, just leave."

Like hell. Jacob wasn't going anywhere until he talked with Shelby. But he didn't have to tell Vaughn that. "Fine, I'll have a drink and then leave."

Vaughn eyed him for a moment and then nodded. "Wise choice."

"No hard feelings?" Jacob asked as he stuck out his hand.

After a second of hesitation, Vaughn smiled and shook his hand, clasping Jacob on his back. "No hard feelings."

Jacob ordered an ice water and took small sips as Vaughn retreated back to the hallway he bounced in. Jacob wasn't going away like a shadow in the night. No, he was going to search this place until he found the man who made his head spin with wonderment. He wasn't sure he was making the wisest choice, but then again, when did Jacob ever do anything that made sense? Not for as long as he could remember.

Taking his glass with him, Jacob slowly made his way upstairs, watching the men around the club. He moved toward the booths and then took a seat at one. His eyes scanned over every face on the dance floor, but didn't see Shelby among the dancers. After about ten minutes, he got up and slowly walked back to the rooms he saw at the back of the second floor.

He checked each one. Aside from finding out that they were bedrooms, he didn't find Shelby. Jacob walked back downstairs. He knew, or really hoped, that Shelby wouldn't be in the back hallway where the BDSM rooms were, so he took the hallway to the right of the bar, finding that there was only one door this time.

Checking over his shoulder to make sure he wasn't followed, Jacob turned the knob and peeked in. He spotted Shelby sitting on a leather couch to his right. Shutting the door behind him, Jacob cleared his throat.

"What are you doing here?" Shelby squeaked as his head shot up.

The man didn't look frightened of Jacob. That was a good thing. He could work with anything else just as long as Shelby wasn't afraid of him. "Looking for you."

* * * *

Shelby had to stop himself from drooling. The man was simply gorgeous. He almost forgot why he was pushing Jacob away. Sitting here now, staring at Jacob, all Shelby could think about was how much he wanted to get closer to the human.

"You shouldn't be in here. This is the prince's office." Even as the words left Shelby's lips, he wanted to take them back. He didn't want Jacob to leave, but he was terrified that Taras would make good on his promise and hurt him or Jacob. Vampires were ten times stronger than humans, and the thought of Jacob being hurt made Shelby feel sick to his stomach.

"If you really want me to leave, I will. But tell me why you are sending me away."

If only it were that easy. Shelby wanted to tell Jacob everything. He wanted to let his mate know that he was a vampire, that he lived off of blood, that he was Jacob's mate. And he wanted to tell Jacob of the threat Taras held over him.

But Shelby was afraid.

He was afraid that Jacob wouldn't accept any of this and run away from him. And Shelby knew that it was becoming harder to resist the man, even after only one night of barely speaking to him. Jacob's closeness did something to Shelby that made his insides quiver.

Sending him away last night took every ounce of restraint Shelby possessed. Sending him away tonight would be impossible.

Shelby's breath caught in his throat as Jacob moved closer, his steps slow and measured. His eyes locked onto Jacob's light-brown ones, his breaths coming in short pants as the man reached the couch. Shelby sat there motionless as Jacob sat down next to him.

Shelby could tell that Jacob wasn't trying to be seductive, but the man had a natural propensity for it. It seemed to ooze from his very pores, and Shelby wanted to fall into the man's arms and inhale Jacob's scent until his lungs were swimming in the fragrance.

"Tell me, Shelby. Why are you pushing me away?"

Oh, yeah. He could listen to the deep rasp of Jacob's voice all night and beg for more come morning light. It was sensual, erotic, and damn sexy.

"Because, my world isn't safe for you," Shelby confessed.

"This club?" Jacob asked as he leaned his head closer, tiny tickles of his breath caressing Shelby's face. He nodded, his lips parting as Shelby leaned closer. He licked his lips, dying to taste his mate for the very first time.

"I think I can hold my own, Shelby," Jacob whispered across Shelby's lips. His expression was so sexually tight that Shelby swallowed several times. Jacob slanted his lips, the tips of his fingers touching Shelby's face as Jacob kissed him for the very first time.

Shelby's body immediately recognized its mate. His pulse began to beat out of control as his fangs ached to sink into Jacob's flesh. He was lost in Jacob's touch, his scent, and his hunger. Jacob took the kiss deeper, licking across Shelby's lips until Shelby opened, and then Jacob plunged in, the rasp of his tongue exploring Shelby's mouth.

A whimpering cry of pleasure filled the air around them as he pushed closer to Jacob, wanting more, wanting it all. Shelby grabbed Jacob's leather, pulling his mate closer, but it still didn't feel close enough. He wanted to be so close to his mate that no one would be able to tell them apart.

He almost shouted a protest when Jacob pulled away, taking his soft and delicious lips with him.

"So, will you go out with me?" Jacob asked as Shelby panted. The man was asking him something, and Shelby couldn't manage to connect two brain cells together at the moment.

He licked his lips once more in remembrance of the hot and sizzling kiss he had just been given. He never knew kissing could be so explosive. He'd been kissed before, but it was never mind-altering. "Yes."

"Are you working tonight?" Jacob asked as he ran the pads of his fingers across Shelby's lips. Shelby's tongue snaked out, tasting the salty skin of his mate.

"No." It seemed all he could give were monosyllables at the moment. Jacob had stolen any ability Shelby had for a higher thought pattern. He was simply going to ride along on yes and no answers.

Jacob grinned and Shelby even forgot the monosyllables. The man was stealing his very breath away. Shelby had always longed for his mate. He had been on the lookout since he was old enough to know what a mate was and what it meant to have one. Now that he knew who his mate was, Shelby was enraptured.

"Do you want to just hang around here?" Jacob teased, as if he knew Shelby was in some sort of trance. He blinked his eyes a few times, trying his best to regroup his mind beyond Jacob. Shelby cleared his throat, feeling a tad embarrassed that he had fallen so hard into Jacob's touches.

"We could." *Thank god I can think again.* "I can introduce you to the members."

"Members? Just exactly what kind of club is this, Shelby?" Jacob asked as he pushed his fingers through Shelby's short hair.

Shelby stiffened. "Just your normal, everyday, spank-you-until-you-beg club." Shelby wanted to smack his forehead. It seemed his brain wasn't fully functional just yet because he was embarrassing the hell out of himself. Why didn't he just tell Jacob that he was a vampire who wanted to bite Jacob until his mate came in his pants?

Jacob's brow arched as he grinned. Shelby could feel himself sinking deeper into the hole he was digging for himself. That was *not* what he had intended to say.

"Then let's check the place out." Jacob stood, holding his hand out for Shelby. Sighing inwardly, Shelby stood and grabbed Jacob's hand, praying his foot didn't lodge any deeper into his big mouth.

Walking from the office, Shelby took the lead and led Jacob to the bar. "Winston, Jimmy, this is my *friend*, Jacob Marshall."

Shelby watched as Jimmy and Winston shook Jacob's hand. "Nice to meet you," Winston said with a smile. The vampire didn't fool Shelby. He was sizing Jacob up. Shelby was going to give Winston a piece of his mind later…much, much later. The guy was huge!

Next Shelby introduced Jacob to Harley, the bouncer and club mind scrubber at the front door. As they were walking away, Harley lifted his hand as if he were going to scrub Jacob's mind. Shelby gave him a hard glare, and Harley chuckled as he winked at Shelby, lowering his hand.

"Just messing around, buddy," Harley said as they walked away.

Shelby introduced him to the bouncers who worked the dance floor, Hudson and Sutton, and Jersey who sometimes pitched in. He knew he didn't need to introduce his mate to Vaughn. Those two knew each other already.

Shelby could feel his body tense and his nervousness take over when Christo and Isla walked their way. Those two were very important men. Christo was Christian's second-in-command, and Isla was his third.

"Christo." The second grabbed Jacob's hand and shook it, a wide smile crossing his lips. "I hear you're Shelby's mate."

Shelby smacked a hand over his face, pushing down the urge to kick Christo.

"His what?" Jacob asked as he looked from Christo to Shelby in confusion.

"Friend," Shelby swiftly supplied.

Christo quirked a brow, but Shelby quickly grabbed Jacob and pulled him away. If Jacob was going to find out Shelby was a vampire, it wasn't going to happen in casual conversation on the dance floor.

* * * *

Jacob had a feeling there was more going on around this place than Shelby was telling him. He had just met the guy, so he wasn't going to push for answers…yet. But he knew that Christo's reference to *mate* did not mean *friend*. The man had looked a little too pleased when he had asked the question.

Even though his gut was telling him something on a deeper level was going on here, Jacob was having a good time. The people seemed fairly nice, although some of the men were a little reserved when Shelby introduced Jacob to them.

As he stood there talking with Emilio, Jacob's head swooned with black waves of dizziness. He knew he needed to sit down and rest for a moment. He excused himself as he made his way to the bar and took a seat, grabbing a napkin from the counter to wipe at his brows.

"Is something wrong?" Shelby asked as he sat next to Jacob, concern marring his black-as-midnight eyes.

"Just a little hot in here," he lied. He just met Shelby and didn't want to scare the man off by telling him he had a rare blood disorder, even if the lie tasted foul on his tongue. "Just let me rest a moment, and then we can dance."

"You dance?" Shelby asked excitedly.

"Yes," Jacob answered with a chuckle. "I like to dance."

"Winston, can you get Jacob an ice water?" Shelby asked the bartender. Jacob was grateful for that small show of kindness. He thanked Winston when the bartender slid him the glass. He took a large swallow of the clear liquid, feeling the water immediately quench his thirst.

"Are you sure you're okay?" Shelby inquired once more. Jacob wasn't going to continue to lie to the man, so he sat the glass down and grinned.

"Let's dance."

Shelby didn't look quite convinced, so Jacob grabbed his hand and pulled the small man onto the dance floor before Shelby could protest. Jacob grabbed Shelby's hips, smiling down at the guy as his hips began to sway back and forth to the music that filled the club.

"I like the way you dance." Shelby gave Jacob a small smile as he placed his hands on Jacob's chest.

"You haven't seen anything yet." Jacob's voice had dropped low. The huskiness was like a soft caress on the wind as he touched Shelby's face again. Shelby shuddered. Jacob just couldn't seem to stop touching the man. His fingers were drawn to the feel of Shelby beneath them. The softness of his skin, the smoothness and texture, was becoming addictive.

Jacob placed one hand on the middle of Shelby's back as he grabbed Shelby's hand with his other, moving him across the floor as if they were the only two in the club. Shelby's midnight-black eyes stayed locked on Jacob's as the lights flashed all around them.

His vision tunneling, Jacob felt as though he were basking in Shelby, in the warmth of his ever-present smile and his hypnotic eyes. He twirled Shelby, making the man laugh loudly as he was pulled back to the safety of Jacob's body.

"I don't think we're dancing appropriately for this song," Shelby pointed out right before Jacob dipped the man backward. Jacob placed a kiss on Shelby's neck before pulling him back up.

"I'm dancing to the song that's beating in my heart for only you."

Shelby gaped at him as Jacob grinned, dancing around the room with Shelby tightly in his arms. He could see his future in Shelby. It was right there in his dark eyes. Jacob could see forever with him.

"No one has ever talked to me that way."

Jacob leaned forward, placing his forehead against Shelby's, taking in Shelby's unique scent. "Get used to it, honey." Jacob swung Shelby wide as he hitched his hips from side to side and then pulled Shelby back to him.

Shelby threw his head back as he laughed and Jacob fell in love with the man in that perfect second. He curled his fingers on the guy's back and pulled Shelby close, taking the man's lips with his, feeling his body heat up as Shelby's tongue snaked out, sending shivers of desires racing through Jacob.

Jacob felt Shelby stiffen, his lips becoming hard as Shelby jerked away from him, staring at the club entrance.

"Let me show you around some more," Shelby quickly said as he pulled Jacob through the crowd and down a hallway where Jacob spotted Vaughn. When Shelby ran into one of the rooms, Jacob saw the surprised look on Vaughn's face just before Shelby slammed the door closed.

Jacob glanced around the room and wondered what in the hell was going on. He hadn't taken Shelby for the kind of guy to have a spanking kink, and from the looks of the room, so much more.

"Is there something you're trying to tell me?"

Shelby swallowed as he looked up at Jacob. "Why would you ask that?"

"Because," Jacob began as he waved his hand around the room, "you've just pulled me into a playroom."

Chapter Three

Dante watched as Christian paced leisurely back and forth in his office. It was becoming a damn headache going on these little field trips with the prince. Granted, he knew how important it was that Christian made sure his twin brothers lay undisturbed, but going to that cold and barren place always made Dante frigid. It took him hours to warm up after one of their visits. And he still wasn't too pleased at having a blindfold wrapped around his damn head.

"I need to find a way to seal their resting place so the elders cannot find them. I am aware that these trips are tiring, but we both know the consequences if they are freed. As of now, it only takes two vampires to open my brothers' resting place. There are three elders," Christian said and then smirked at Dante. "You do the math."

Dante knew full well the consequences if Ceri or Rhys were freed. "Have you tried to reach out and sense where the elders are?"

"Time and again." Christian sighed heavily. "But something is blocking them. I can't get a reading on them, and that worries me."

A worried prince was not a good thing in Dante's opinion. He stood, walking around his desk as he placed his hand on Christian's shoulder. "Then let's go check on your brothers. We'll come up with some way to ensure that the elders do not find them."

Christian nodded, gratitude in his eyes as he blindfolded Dante and then they disseminated.

* * * *

Shelby swallowed as he glanced around the room. It hadn't been his intention to come into one of the playrooms, but he had spotted Taras and felt panicked to get away.

The last thing Shelby wanted was for Taras to know he had a mate. That was exactly why Shelby had sent Jacob away. But did his mate stay away?

No.

"I meant to go down the other hallway. The one with the prince's office," Shelby said as he inched back toward the door. He just prayed Taras was gone.

Why in the hell had the vampire come back? Was he out to torture Shelby? The man said he would be around when Shelby fell. Did that include finding his mate?

Shelby was so damn confused and scared. He needed to get Jacob out of here and go home. He shouldn't have even come here tonight.

"I'm not feeling too well. Can we do this another night?"

"What, play?" Jacob looked shocked and Shelby wanted to growl. That was not what he meant.

"No, I mean see each other."

Jacob didn't look too happy, but gave a short nod. "If that's what you want."

No, that was not what Shelby wanted. He wanted Taras to leave him the hell alone. He wanted Jacob to take him and claim him—preferably not in this room.

Jacob opened the door, giving Shelby one last look before he walked out, shutting the door behind him.

Shelby sighed as he disseminated to his bedroom at the manor. He undressed, showered, and then crawled into bed, praying Jacob wasn't upset about the abrupt ending of their wonderful night.

Shelby lay in his bed, closing his eyes as he wrapped his hand around his cock. With his other hand, he touched his lips, remembering the kisses that were placed there. Jacob was one hell of a kisser, making Shelby forget to breathe.

He began a slow and relaxed pace, thinking of Jacob holding him close as they danced, as his hand moved up and down his cock. He was so used to men trying to grope him when he danced that Shelby had been surprised Jacob hadn't tried anything like that. The man honestly wanted to dance with him.

He began to imagine Jacob's kiss traveling further down his heated flesh, peppering kisses and lapping his tongue over his body. Shelby's skin tingled as he arched his back, moaning as his thumb traced across the head of his cock, gathering the clear liquid as Jacob's hands slid down his body, touching Shelby in every intimate spot he possessed.

Shelby rolled to his knees, keeping his hand on his cock as he reached back and rolled his tight sac in his other hand. He imagined Jacob behind him, lapping at his hole as Shelby pleaded uselessly for Jacob to fuck him.

Rocking back and forth, Shelby let small, helpless whimpers fall from his lips as he reached even further back, tracing his hole with his fingers as he stroked his cock. "Jacob," he cried as one finger slid inside of him.

Oh god, why couldn't it be Jacob's finger? Shelby wanted it to be Jacob's finger so badly. He rocked his body back until his finger was fully inside of him as he began to stroke his cock harder.

Sliding another finger into his ass, Shelby saw Jacob laying his body over Shelby's, planting kisses down his back as he whispered sweet words to him. In the darkness of his bedroom, Shelby allowed his fangs to bite into his bottom lip as a third finger joined the other two.

"I want you, Jacob," Shelby whispered as he squeezed the head of his cock in his fist before sliding his hand down his shaft and pulling on his dick once more. It wasn't enough. It would never be enough unless it was his mate doing things to Shelby's body that he had only dreamed of, only done to himself.

Shelby cried out in frustration as he fucked his fingers and jerked on his cock. He needed release in the worst way. His body was on fire for Jacob, and the man was nowhere in sight. His back bowed as Shelby shouted Jacob's name to the shadows of the night, spilling his seed into his hand, feeling the cold creep in as the high of his orgasm ebbed away.

Shelby removed his hand and collapsed on his bed, feeling just as lonely as he had when he first crawled into bed. He used the towel on his nightstand to clean his hand before pulling the covers over his body. Shelby grabbed one of his pillows and cradled it in his arms, letting his mind imagine that it was Jacob he was holding.

One night soon it would be Jacob in his bed. Shelby held on to that hope as he closed his eyes.

* * * *

"I want you and Isla to check the sewer system under the city."

Christo scratched his chin as he listened to Christian. He had heard from the prince that the rogues were starting to form a subcommunity down in the sewers. Christo wasn't too sure he wanted to go down there to say hello, though.

Knocking on rogues' doors wasn't the smartest thing in the world to do. "And if we spot any?"

"Then you report back to me what you find," Christian said as he stood. "Don't try and take any of them on. From my understanding, they are uniting. If one attacks, I'm almost sure reinforcements will follow."

"And here I thought you liked me," Christo said as he stood.

"You are my second, Christo. I trust no one with this job but you and Isla. I am well aware of the allures of the dark side of our species, but trust you two will resist the temptation."

"Hmm, do I really want to resist becoming a mindless killer?"

"Get out of here." Christian grinned and then sobered. "Be careful, Christo. I'm not sure how deep the problem goes."

"I'll try to keep my ass from getting torn apart," Christo said as he left the office in search of Isla. As usual, he found his best friend on the dance floor, freaking on some human.

Christo slapped Isla's arm with the back of his hand. "We have to roll out, bro."

Isla glared at Christo from over his shoulder. "I think you get off on pulling me away from donors."

"Hardly." Christo chuckled as he walked toward the door. "But Christian did give us an assignment to handle."

Isla caught up with Christo, a curious expression on his face. "Where is he sending us?"

Christo fought the smile on his lips as he pointed to a manhole cover a foot away from them. "Down there."

Isla looked from the iron lid to Christo. "Are you nuts? He wants us to go down into the sewer?"

"Yep, and you can go first," Christo said as he pulled the lid free and set it aside, smirking up at Isla. "Ladies first."

"Not on your life," Isla replied as he took a step forward, staring down into the manhole.

"Pussy?" Christo chided before standing and then dropping down into the underbelly of the city, landing on his feet. He took a step forward, giving Isla room. He heard his best friend drop into the sewer behind him a moment later.

Christo glanced around, opening his senses to the scourge of the vampire world. "We are only to witness the quantity of rogues down here, Isla."

"No worries there. I know how to spot and run."

Christo grinned. As scared as Isla was behaving, he knew for a fact that Isla Cordone was a deadly opponent. The man had fought in the vampire wars five hundred years ago, coming out victorious. He didn't fool Christo.

The water trickled down the walls as a small conduit of foul-smelling water took up the middle of the passageway, working its way through the dimly lit sewer. The black water looked totally disgusting as Christo skirted around it. The air was cool, and it clung to his face and hands. Christo reached out to steady himself but quickly moved his hand away from the slimy and mildew-ridden wall. He was going to need a deep-cleansing shower after this trip.

His foot stilled when he spotted rats scurrying by. "Why in the fuck do rats have to live in the sewer?"

"Who's the pussy now?" Isla teased as he walked past Christo and began to lead the way. Just because Christo was a vampire didn't mean he liked rats. The foul little vermin were just…He shivered and moved by them.

Their steps were silent, their movements swift as the two checked the vast branches of tunnels of the underground sewer system. Isla stilled. Christo cocked his head, listening. He could hear movement ahead of them. Rogues were not as quiet as they would hope to be. Their steps were marked with noise, carelessness. They were only out to hunt, uncaring that they were not stealthily quiet.

"How many?" Christo asked under his breath for only Isla to hear.

His friend glanced back at Christo, a grim frown on his face as he shook his head. Fuck, this was not good. They were going to have to get closer in order to see. Isla began to move, Christo following as they turned into another tunnel.

Christo froze.

He reached out and grabbed Isla's arm just as the rogues behind them attacked. How the hell did they creep up so quietly on the two? He heard Isla curse as he fought one of the rogues in front of him. Christo could see more heading their way. He couldn't understand why the rogues were helping each other. They were solitary creatures, preferring to hunt on their own. And now they were coming to each other's aid? Something wasn't right about any of this.

Christo kicked out, dislodging the vampire from his side as he once again grabbed Isla and disseminated right into Christian's office.

"We have a problem."

* * * *

Jacob licked his lips in nervousness as he entered the club. He had made dinner reservations for himself and Shelby. He knew the man had sun allergies, so he made the reservations for just after dusk. Shelby had told Jacob that he didn't work tonight, so there shouldn't be any problems.

As he walked into the club, Jacob immediately spotted Shelby sitting up on the second floor, surrounded by a few men. He looked to be laughing and having a good time. Jacob thought Shelby the most handsome man when he smiled. He had deep dimples on both sides of his cheeks that gave him that boyish charming look.

Seeing those pearly whites made Jacob's cock hard as he walked up the stairs to the second-floor balcony. He stood there fascinated for a moment as he heard Shelby's musical voice above the others, the inflection light.

Leaning against the railing, Jacob just watched the man as he talked. He realized that he could do this for hours. Shelby enchanted him. When the man's dark eyes rose and locked onto Jacob, it felt as though electricity began to shoot between them. Shelby smiled as he pushed away from the booth, heading Jacob's way.

"Evening," Jacob said as Shelby stopped in front of him.

"Hi." Shelby smiled.

"I made dinner reservations for the two of us. If I remember correctly, you have tonight off, *and* it's dark outside." Jacob watched as the smile slowly slid from Shelby's face, his sparkling eyes dimming. Did he say something wrong?

"I can't go," Shelby said as he glanced past Jacob.

"Can't?" Jacob probed. "What do you mean you can't go?" Everything had been planned perfectly. Shelby didn't have to work, it was dark outside, and Jacob had even remembered to bring an extra helmet and riding jacket. What was the problem?

"I can't go," Shelby repeated as he finally lifted his gaze to Jacob. "Please understand."

"I don't understand, Shelby," Jacob said as he tried his damnedest to keep the hurt and anger out of his tone. "Explain to me why you can't walk out of here right now and join me for dinner."

Shelby took a step back, his hands wringing in front of him. "The prince says I can't leave the club with you."

Jacob felt his back molars gnashing as he stared down at Shelby. Of all the lame excuses the man could give him, he used the prince? He was starting to get a clearer picture here. Was Shelby even allergic to the sun, or was that another excuse to brush Jacob off? It seemed every time he tried to get Shelby to go somewhere with him, there was a ready excuse.

"If you don't want to be seen with me, be man enough to admit it. You are a grown man, Shelby. No one is stopping you from leaving except you." Jacob spun on his heel, jogging down the steps and heading straight of the door. He wasn't going to beg the man to do a damn thing. If Shelby didn't want to be seen with him, fine.

It still stung like hell, though. He was well aware of the tattoos littering his arms, of the rough look he carried. But Jacob wasn't going to change who he was for anyone. Not even the handsome little man who had wormed his way into Jacob's heart.

* * * *

Shelby stood there stunned. Jacob thought he didn't want to be seen with him? Oh god, what had he done? Shelby wanted to shout to the world that Jacob was his. He wasn't embarrassed to be seen with the man.

Quickly running down the steps, Shelby left Connor, Eli, and Yasuko sitting in the booth to stare at him strangely as he headed for Christian's office. He had to explain things to his mate. Shelby couldn't let the man think that he was ashamed of him.

Thank god he knew for a fact Christian wasn't in his office at the moment. Shelby had seen the prince over by Vaughn in the BDSM hallway.

He wasn't sure where to look. Shelby didn't have a clue where Jacob lived. But he had heard Vaughn talk about some club called The Fox's Den where he and Tiny used to hang out. Shelby wondered briefly why Jacob was called Tiny. The man was anything but. He pushed the boggling thought from his mind as he concentrated on the street outside.

If he knew where the club was, he could disseminate right to it, but as it was, Shelby would have to ask around. He shivered as he appeared on the sidewalk in front of The Manacle, praying that Christian didn't find out he had left.

It was bad enough he was defying the prince. Christian was a very protective coven leader. But Christian's patience with Shelby wasn't endless. To defy him was punishable. And even though Shelby was well loved by the prince, he wouldn't receive immunity.

That meant he had to haul ass.

Why hadn't he at least taken a small taste of Jacob? It would have made finding him a lot easier. He could have used the blood call to track Jacob down. Now all he could do was go on foot and guess at where his mate was.

He asked a few strangers and was finally pointed in the right direction. Shelby stood outside a less-than-friendly-looking bar. There were motorcycles lined up in a row out front, and the place looked menacing, uninviting.

But Shelby had to convince Jacob that the situation between them wasn't what his mate thought. Shelby knew he was going to have to tell Jacob about vampires and the prince if he was going to make the human understand. He just prayed Jacob didn't wash his hands of Shelby.

Pushing the door open, Shelby stepped into a low-lit bar. The stench of cigarettes and alcohol hit his nostrils hard, almost making him gag. Waving his hand in front his nose, Shelby spotted the bar and walked over to it, praying he didn't smell of the stench once he left. He scooted onto a barstool, staring at the back of the bartender's head, waiting to be acknowledged.

"What do we have here?" a thick and tattooed man asked as he sat down next to Shelby. The guy may have been built like Jacob, but the man could use a good shower and a dentist. He had a scraggly beard as well that looked like he kept crumbs for snacks inside of it.

"I'm looking for Jacob. Have you seen him?"

"Who?" the man asked as he rested an arm on the counter.

Oh yeah. Jacob didn't go by that name here. Shelby had forgotten. "Tiny."

The man laughed as he slapped his hand on the counter, glancing around the room. "He says he's looking for Tiny."

Shelby looked behind him to see at least five men standing, heading his way. He wasn't sure what was going on, but things didn't look in his favor for finding out where Jacob could be. "Have you seen him?"

"And why would a small fellow like you be looking for Tiny?" the man asked curiously. Shelby could tell the man was fucking with him. He sighed. Apparently Jacob wasn't here. Shelby knew in his heart that if Jacob were anywhere in this bar, he would have been out here by now.

"Thank you for your time," Shelby said as he turned to slide off of the stool.

"Where do you think you're going?" the man asked as he grabbed Shelby's arm. "I want to know why you're looking for Tiny."

"I would suggest you take your arm off of me, sir." That was as kind as Shelby was going to get. He may have had a hard time fighting Taras's advances in the back room, but a human he could take on with no problem. Shelby honestly didn't want to go down that route, but if the human left him no choice…

"Do you hear that, men?" The man holding him laughed. "The little guy is warning me to let him go."

"Tiny isn't here," another man volunteered. "And your kind isn't welcome."

His kind? Did these men know Shelby was a vampire? He curled his top lip over his fangs, trying his best to hide them. "I'm going to go now."

The man yanked on Shelby's arm. "Tiny isn't the kind of man who dabbles with little fairies like you, boy."

What did that mean?

"I would suggest you forget you ever met the man. He'd tear your head off for even implying such a thing. Don't get the wrong idea just because someone says a kind word to you." The man squeezed Shelby's arm harder, painfully. "You got that?"

Shelby blew out a steady breath as he tried his best not to hurt these men. "Let. Go. Of. My. Arm."

The six men laughed as the one holding Shelby jerked his arm painfully back.

He had warned them.

Shelby was lightning quick as the other hand came around to smash the human's nose, blood pouring from his face as he released Shelby to grab his nose. "You little prick."

Slipping underneath the Neanderthals, Shelby ran quickly to the door. He hadn't come here to fight, and he wasn't sure how thankful Jacob would be if he hurt his friends. Shelby ran outside and around the building to disseminate, only to be knocked to the ground.

This was not turning out to be his night.

Getting quickly to his feet, Shelby cursed under his breath when he saw two vampire rogues standing there before him. He knew he was about to get his ass handed to him. Maybe it would have been better if he had defied Christian and went out to dinner with Jacob. At least he could have gotten fucked instead of fucked up.

"A snack." One of the rogues laughed as he lunged for Shelby. He spun around to avoid the man tackling him when he was kicked in his side. Shelby went down, hard. That was going to leave a damn bruise.

Jumping to his feet, Shelby jumped onto one of the rogues, biting deeply into the vampire's neck, feeling the wretched taste of tainted blood on his tongue as he tried to tear the damn thing's neck out.

He was jerked away, hitting the ground on his back, knocking the wind out of him. Shelby didn't have time to think. He rolled away just as the rogue vampire tried to stab him. Oh shit, the vampire had a fucking silver knife.

Shelby saw the wooden handle and swallowed hard right before the vampire he had bitten smacked him dead across his face. Shelby's head snapped back, but he managed to stay upright. He leapt again, sinking his teeth in deep as he yanked his head back and forth.

Shelby was never comfortable biting into flesh, but if it saved his life, he'd bite every damn rogue out there.

The rogue howled as Shelby tore the bastard's throat out. He knew he couldn't take on two rogues, but one was going down if he was. Shelby may be slight in build and on the short side for a vampire, but Christian, Christo, and Isla had taught him well on how to defend himself. Too bad he hadn't kicked Taras's ass that day in The Manacle.

Being caught off guard and threatened hadn't helped him. Taras was a lot stronger than he looked. And Shelby hadn't been fighting for his life that day either. Now he was fighting not only for his life, but to get back to his mate.

If Jacob ever forgave him.

When something hard hit him on the back of his head, Shelby knew he had to get the hell out of there. He had been lucky with the bastard he had killed. But luck wasn't going to smile down on him twice. And as much as he didn't like those men inside the bar, he couldn't chance one of them stumbling out here and getting killed.

Jumping from the dead rogue, Shelby quickly disseminated to the club. Unfortunately, he hadn't thought of the prince's office. He appeared right next to the bar, bloody and bruised, and swaying slightly.

"Shit!" Winston shouted as he ran around the bar, grabbing Shelby up into his arms and carrying him down the hallway to Christian's office. He knew he looked a mess. The rogue's blood covered the entire front of his shirt and his neck and face. His ribs were killing him as well.

"What happened?" The prince growled out the question as Winston laid Shelby on the leather couch. Damn, his body was sore as hell.

"I don't know. He just appeared in front of the bar looking like this."

Christian knelt in front of Shelby, lifting Shelby's shirt and then clenching his jaw. "Who did this to you, Shelby?"

He was so fucked.

Chapter Four

Jacob felt like an ass. He had stormed out of the club without thinking of Shelby. He knew in his heart that Shelby wasn't the type of man to be hung up on appearances, and the man's kiss had proven just how much he wanted Jacob.

With his tail tucked between his legs, Jacob walked back into the club.

He glanced around when he saw people packed over by the bar, excited voices filling the air around him. Jacob didn't know the people Shelby worked with too well. He had just been introduced, but the bartender, Winston, seemed kind of nice—even if Jacob had thought of him as the wax man. Jacob pushed past the crowd as he waved Winston over. "What's going on?"

"Follow me," Winston said as he walked from behind the bar. Jacob once again pushed his way through the crowd as he followed Winston down the hallway that contained the prince's office. He frowned when the bartender opened the office door, waving Jacob inside.

Jacob crossed the room in long, angry strides as he saw Shelby lying on the couch, a bloody mess. A low, threatening growl rumbled inside of him when he saw the bruise marring Shelby's face. "What happened to him?"

The prince—he gave up on trying to call the man anything else—stood, his jaw tensing. "It seems Shelby disobeyed me and left the club."

"What are you, his father?" Jacob snapped in anger. So Shelby was telling the truth. Didn't he feel like a rank jackass?

"Close enough," the prince said as he glowered at Jacob. "Was he with you?"

Damn, what did the guy mean *close enough*? Jacob was confused as hell, and only getting more confused as the night wore on.

"I swear, Prince, Jacob had nothing to do with this. I mean, he wasn't with me," Shelby defended as he tried to sit up. Jacob immediately pressed Shelby back down to the sofa. The man looked like he was in a lot of pain. He tried to study Shelby's face for any signs of where the blood had come from, but he didn't see any cuts or gashes, and a bloody nose wouldn't have produced so much blood.

"You are to go to the manor and stay there until I figure out your punishment," the prince said as he walked over to his desk, anger evident in his dark eyes.

"Wait," Jacob said as he stood, holding his hand up in front of him. "I understand that Shelby disobeyed you. But he's a grown man. I don't think—"

"It would be wise if you didn't," the prince said as his face began to evolve into something truly frightening. It darkened until the man didn't resemble a damn human any longer. "He may be your mate, but until you take full responsibility for him, he is under my care."

Jacob was so fucking lost.

"Then can I go with him?" Jacob asked as he walked back over to Shelby and stood in front of him. "I will make sure he doesn't leave the manor."

The man sighed as he dropped down into his chair, looking years older in a span of a minute. He waved his hand, and the next thing Jacob knew, he was standing in some sort of bedroom.

What the hell was going on?

Jacob spun around when he heard sheets rustling. Shelby was trying to get up. As bizarre as things were around him now, Jacob wasn't going to let Shelby stand on his own two feet. The man didn't look like he could lie on his own back.

"Where are you trying to go?" he asked as he helped the small man sit up.

"I need a shower," Shelby said as he waved a hand down at his body. "If you can't tell, I'm covered in blood."

Not only could Jacob tell, but he could smell it as well. Was blood supposed to smell that god-awful? "Let me help you." Jacob helped Shelby pull his shirt over his head, trying his best not to openly ogle the man. But that thought was quickly replaced by rage when he saw the dark bruises on Shelby's ribs. "Who did this to you?"

Shelby pushed from the bed, his fingers fighting to unfasten his pants. "No one you know, I promise."

That wasn't good enough for Jacob, but he wasn't going to argue the point right now. He helped the man the rest of the way out of his clothes, swallowing tightly as he glanced away. Shelby was even more beautiful than Jacob had imagined. And he had imagined a lot in the past two nights.

He undressed and then grabbed Shelby, taking him to the bathroom. The man didn't protest. He didn't look like he could stand on his own right now. Jacob started the shower and then stepped under the spray.

"I'm sorry," Shelby whispered as Jacob began to wash the blood from Shelby's face.

"For what, Shelby?"

"For making you think I was ashamed of you," he answered weakly.

"We'll discuss it later." Jacob leaned Shelby back, letting the water wash over his hair when he saw the sharp fangs in Shelby's mouth. Jacob stared at the sharp, gleaming white teeth for a space of moments and then finished washing Shelby down.

He knew the man's secret now. And knowing Shelby's secret made everything else fit together much better than it had before. It now made sense for the prince to be called prince. It also made a hell of a lot of sense to him why The Manacle seemed so dark, so foreboding.

It was a vampire club.

Once he had Shelby washed down and blood-free, Jacob carried the man to the bed. Shelby stayed silent the whole time, watching Jacob closely. As if he knew Jacob had guessed his little secret.

There was no way Shelby could know this, so Jacob gently laid the man down. "How do you feel?" Jacob pressed softly at the bruises purpling at Shelby's side. He knew they hurt like hell.

"They'll heal," Shelby said as he rolled to his side, his soft cock lying against his left hip. The sight made Jacob all too aware that he was standing there naked as well. He glanced down at the floor where his clothes lay, but knowing the last thing he wanted to do was put them back on.

Sliding onto the bed, Jacob pulled Shelby into his arms. He was afraid. Jacob wasn't too big a man to admit that. He was holding a vampire in his arms. But so far Shelby had proven to be nothing but a sweet and meek man.

"You're shaking," Shelby pointed out as he pressed his back into Jacob's chest. "Why are you shaking?"

Jacob hadn't realized he was shaking, but now that Shelby had pointed that fact out, he noticed a slight shiver in his body. "It's cold."

"You're not a very good liar," Shelby stated blandly. "And I don't like being lied to."

Jacob released the breath burning in his lungs as he rolled to his back, staring up at the very pristine ceiling. "I've never held a vampire in my arms before, happy?"

"Thrilled," Shelby said as he turned over. "How did you guess?"

Jacob could see not only curiosity in the man's eyes, but an undercurrent of fear. Seeing how uncertain Shelby was went a long way in soothing Jacob. The man almost looked too terrified to speak.

"Your fangs."

Shelby curled his fingers in as he broke eye contact and glanced down the bed. "Are you going to leave me now?"

"Depends," Jacob answered honestly. He wasn't going to lie. Apparently the little vamp could smell, taste, feel, or whatever he did to know Jacob was lying. "Are you going to do anything bad to me?"

Shelby rose to his knees quickly, his head shaking back and forth. "I would never hurt you, Jacob. You're my mate."

There went that word again. "Does that mean we're it for each other?" After all, he did watch Animal Planet, and Jacob was smarter than the average bear. Shelby's eyes widened, and then a smile tipped his lips up at the corner, but not enough to show off his stunning dimples.

Too bad.

"I knew you were smart." Shelby said it almost proudly.

Jacob was even more confused, but he let the subject go for now. He was getting a headache. "How do you feel?"

"Fine," Shelby stated. "I'll heal by morning."

Must be nice. "Who did this to you, and why?"

Shelby's smile wilted as he sat back on the bed, looking as if he was about to tell Jacob something he didn't want to hear. And once Shelby had told him what had happened, Jacob was right. Although he was going to pay a visit to The Fox's Den. He never really did like those men.

"Are you mad at me?" Shelby asked as he pulled the end of the sheet into his lap, covering the dark hair that haloed his soft cock.

"I'm not happy," Jacob confessed. He was starting to get a clearer picture of why the prince kept such a tight rein on Shelby. Trouble just seemed to come knocking on the man's door. "Promise me you won't go looking for me again, Shelby."

"I can't," Shelby said. Jacob couldn't fault the man for being honest, but it wasn't the answer he wanted to hear.

"Why can't you promise me to keep yourself safe?"

Shelby's chin jutted out as his hands landed on his bare hips. "Because you are my mate. It is my job to keep you safe and happy. It is also my honor to teach you the ways of my people."

It was as if the man was reciting something instead of telling him what he really thought. He held back the laugh at the thought of Shelby keeping *him* safe. The man was too small to take on a fly. Jacob knew he had his job cut out for him.

"Come here, Mr. Badass." Jacob hooked his hand behind Shelby's neck and pulled his little vamp down to him. Did it freak him out that Shelby was a vampire? Yes. Was he going to show it? No. Jacob was going to see where this led. He had a dark side to him. He knew this. He acknowledged this. And the thought of Jacob feeding from him touched on some deep craving inside of him.

Shelby moved closer, staring down at Jacob as he licked his lips. "Let me see."

"See what?" Shelby asked as he pulled back a few inches.

"Your fangs."

Shelby's palms flattened on Jacob's chest as his lips fluttered and then raised, two sharp points becoming visible. His eyes snapped down to Jacob, as if trying to gauge Jacob's reaction. When Jacob smiled, Shelby's grin showed his dimples. "You like them?"

Jacob nodded as he cupped Shelby's jaw, examining the sharp teeth a little more closely. "How often do you bite with them?" Jacob wasn't sure why he was asking, but something inside of him wanted to know.

"Not often. I drink crimson. I…" Shelby bit into his bottom lip and tried to look away, but Jacob held firm to his jaw. "I don't feed like other vampires. I'm not comfortable with the act of biting into someone's flesh."

A vampire who was squeamish of biting? Jacob released Shelby's jaw and pulled him closer, licking across the man's bottom lip. He could feel small pants of air escaping Shelby's mouth as his breathing became unsteady.

"Afraid?" Jacob asked teasingly.

"Nervous," Shelby admitted.

"Of a kiss?"

"Of what comes after the kiss."

Had Shelby been that sheltered? The thought slowed Jacob down. It damn near made him slam on the brakes. Damn near. "What do you think will follow the kiss?" Jacob asked as he kissed each spot on Shelby's face where he knew the dimples lay.

Shelby's eyelids fluttered. "Sex."

Jacob's hand slid down Shelby's side, around his hip, and rested on the man's back thigh, right below the man's bared cheek. Jacob resisted the urge to let his hand rise higher. He knew with Shelby, things had to progress slowly. He was like a skittish puppy. His body jerked slightly with every move Jacob made.

"Are you afraid of sex, Shelby?" Jacob watched the man's eyes, gauging his reaction this time.

"N–No."

Now who was lying? There was the barest hint of tenseness in Shelby's eyes. Jacob lay still, trying his best to relax the man. He wasn't sure if the kiss was a prelude to sex, but he was going to let things happen naturally.

"No?" Jacob teased as one lone finger swiped across Shelby's small mound. His little vamp shivered. "Then kiss me."

Shelby leaned forward, his lips barely touching Jacob's. It was timid at first, and then Jacob took over, easing the man in. Shelby moaned as he moved closer. Jacob could feel the man's full erection pressing into his stomach. Shelby may be nervous, but he was willing, excited.

"Have you ever sucked cock, Shelby?" Jacob asked as he let his tongue trail along Shelby's bottom lip.

"Is that what you want?"

Jacob noticed that Shelby didn't answer his question, and he also realized in that moment that he didn't want an answer. "Will your fangs get in the way?" He avoided giving an answer as well. Jacob didn't pressure Shelby, didn't push him down toward his cock. Instead, he pulled Shelby up until the small man was perched on his waist.

Shelby looked surprised.

"Kiss me," Jacob said as his hands slid up Shelby's soft skin, his fingers enjoying the satiny smoothness of his pale flesh. The man leaned forward, the kiss a little more confident. Jacob wanted to growl as his cock brushed over Shelby's ass. The sensation sent flames instantly to his groin, making Jacob force the hitch of his hips to still.

Not only was Shelby's tongue exploring Jacob's mouth, but his hands began to move over Jacob's arms, his fingers playing with Jacob's biceps. His little vampire was gaining confidence. Jacob turned, depositing Shelby onto the bed next to him. He turned again. Shelby was now neatly tucked under him.

The kiss hadn't been broken. Shelby held on to Jacob, opening his mouth wider, their tongues dueling. Shock waves ran down Jacob's rib cage when Shelby's hands skated down his chest, heading straight for his cock.

Jacob swallowed as he kissed Shelby, wondering if the vampire was going to be brave enough to touch him. So far the man had seemed afraid of sex, but he was warming up nicely. Jacob held still as Shelby's fingers curved around his cock, giving it a light squeeze. He couldn't stop the moan. He was only human. A male at that.

Jacob began to kiss the soft skin of Shelby's neck as his little vampire's hand squeezed his cock again. He wasn't too sure if Shelby knew what he was doing, and was about to ask that very question when Shelby began to stroke him in all the right ways.

Was there really such a thing as a bad hand job?

Jacob didn't think so. Not the way Shelby was twisting his wrist and smearing Jacob's pre-cum around the head on every upstroke. Damn, the man learned quickly. Jacob glanced down at Shelby's hand, needing to see what his body was so thoroughly enjoying.

When his head tilted sideways to get a better view, Shelby sank his teeth into Jacob's neck, making his cock explode and his eyes widen at the same time.

That, he had not seen coming.

Jacob swallowed hard and took a deep breath. The powerful sensation was still coursing through him as Jacob slowly lowered his eyelids, his breathing evening out as Shelby began to lap at his neck.

The man froze underneath him, as if realizing in that second what he had done. Jacob couldn't talk at the moment to shush Shelby's worries because he was trying to swallow his pulse back into his throat.

It had been that good.

"Jacob, I–I'm sorry."

Sated, Jacob shook his head, endorphins still swimming through his bloodstream, giving him the most pleasure he had ever experienced. At least while not buried deep in some tight ass.

He rolled to his back, his arms and legs shaky as he laid an arm over his eyes, trying his best to enjoy the bliss for as long as he could.

But Shelby had other plans.

"Are you mad at me, Jacob? Please say something. I don't like the silence."

Jacob reached up and laid a finger on Shelby's lips, letting his breath out slowly as the last of the endorphins left his system. "Why would you think I was mad at you, Shelby?"

"Because I bit you," Shelby said from behind Jacob's finger.

"And I crawled into bed with a vampire. If I didn't want to get bitten, I should have put my clothes on and left."

"Good point."

Jacob grinned and removed his finger so Shelby wouldn't sound so muffled when he spoke. His senses were coming back online, and Jacob felt the silk sheets beneath him. He usually wasn't a big fan of silk. Cotton breathed, but silk clung to his body when he sweated.

"Can I ask you something?" Shelby asked as he pulled his legs to his chest.

Jacob really didn't want to have pillow talk right now. He was too busy yawning. That powerful of an orgasm required sleep. That was a law, wasn't it? *It should be.*

"I taste sickness in you. But I'm not a powerful enough vampire to know exactly what it is. What is it?"

Jacob could hear the tension in Shelby's voice. He hadn't thought that Shelby would be able to taste *the sickness* in him, but he hadn't thought once Shelby's sharp fangs sank into his neck, either. "I was diagnosed with a rare blood disorder," he said as he turned over to face his little vampire.

Shelby studied Jacob's face, giving a small nod, his eyes saying that he still didn't understand.

"Can you get it from drinking my blood?" The thought was sudden and scared Jacob. He didn't want to pass this crap on to someone else, least of all Shelby.

"No," Shelby said as he shook his head quickly. "I can't catch human diseases or give them. But it did taste…off."

Yeah, *off* would be a damn good word to use. Everything was off about what Jacob had. The doctors said it was idiopathic, the onset had no apparent cause. "Basically, my body doesn't replenish my blood cells. I have a low count of red blood cells, white blood cells, and platelets. My bone marrow is all screwed up."

"And I took what little you had." Shelby gasped.

"Don't freak out on me, Shelby. I'm cool." Jacob was feeling a little light-headed, but Shelby seemed to be doing a pretty good job freaking out as it was. He wasn't going to add to it.

Jacob grabbed Shelby and pulled the man into his arms, closing his eyes, feeling the tiredness that seemed to accompany him all the time lately coming on. He yawned again and wrapped his arms around his vamp a little tighter.

* * * *

Jacob swallowed his medication down with a glass of orange juice as he let Mango out to use the bathroom. He had hated to leave Shelby this morning, but he hadn't brought his medication with him to the manor.

He stared at the business card held to the refrigerator by a magnet. It was his doctor's card. Jacob had refused to even talk about a bone marrow transplant. He knew the risks, and he didn't feel as though he could deal with the chemotherapy or the entire procedure, period.

But since meeting Shelby, Jacob was seriously considering it. He wanted more time with the small man, wanted to get to know the little vampire better.

Mango barked, wagging his tail as Jacob stared at the square card. The German Shepherd shoved his nose into Jacob's leg as if trying to wake him from his thoughts.

"I see ya, fella." Jacob grabbed the large rawhide bone from the counter and tossed it into the living room, watching Mango chase after the newly purchased bone. Mango was only two, basically still a puppy, and Jacob's best friend.

He grabbed his glass of orange juice, taking it to the living room where he slid down the front of the couch and sat on the carpet, running his hand over Mango's soft furry head. "What do you think, boy? Should I do it?"

Mango looked up at Jacob, as if he understood what his master was asking. He barked once and then licked Jacob's hand.

"You're just saying that because you know I take such good care of you." He petted the dog's head once again as he rested his arm on his bent knee, dangling the glass between his fingers.

Everything about what was going on inside his body scared the hell out of Jacob, but the procedure to *cure* him scared him even more. Even if he gave his doc the go-ahead, a match would have to be found. Family was preferable, but Mango was the only family Jacob had. He didn't think his doctor would approve of a German Shepherd donating his bone marrow.

He tipped the glass to his lips, thinking of Shelby. It wasn't just the small vampire's looks, although he had to admit Shelby was stunning. It was the way he talked, walked, laughed, blushed, and danced. It was the entire package, and Jacob cursed at fate for giving him someone so damn right when things were going so damn wrong.

He got up and placed his glass in the kitchen sink, grabbing the card from the refrigerator, taking his cell phone out and dialing the number.

* * * *

Jacob had spent most of the morning on the phone with his doctor and then slept the afternoon away. By the time he got up and took care of Mango, nightfall was here. He decided to go to the club.

If Shelby was still on house arrest, he would drive out that way. Leaving the manor this morning gave him the location, and he knew he wouldn't have problems finding it. He needed to get Shelby a phone. It would have been a lot simpler just to call.

Since he lived closer to the club than the manor, he headed that way first. As he swung his leg over his bike, he noticed someone standing between two parked cars in the parking lot, glaring at him.

Jacob didn't scare easily. If the little punk wanted some, he could come get it. The man didn't look familiar, but Jacob couldn't remember every enemy he had made. He sat his helmet on his bike and then took his leather off.

He would need the swinging room just in case the little punk grew balls.

"You are Shelby's mate?" the man asked with a sugary tone. Jacob didn't trust that tone, especially since the man had just been glaring at him a second ago.

"Who wants to know?"

Jacob didn't even have a chance to blink before the man was in front of him, shoving the palm of his hand into Jacob's chest. He hit the ground hard, but jumped back up just as quickly. His sternum hurt, but Jacob pushed the pain aside.

"Tell Shelby Taras visited you," the man said before his arm came barreling at Jacob at lightning speed. He managed to jump back just in time and noticed that he was getting pretty damn winded.

This was not good.

Jacob blocked the next blow, and the next one after that, his energy expended to the point he was almost panting. He was in shape. He wasn't that old. But with the disease coursing through his veins, it seemed fighting was too much.

The man got off another shot, knocking Jacob clean on his ass once more. It dawned on Jacob while he pulled himself off the ground that his fighting days were over—which meant he couldn't even defend Shelby if push came to shove. And he was pretty sure in the vampire world, one would need to know how to fight to survive.

It didn't bother him so much that his badass days were gone. It happened. What bothered Jacob was the knowledge that he couldn't protect his little vampire if it came down to it.

"Stay down, mutt," Taras said as he used that lightning-quick move again to slam Jacob up against someone's car. "Tell him I haven't forgotten and he will pay for what he had done to me."

"What did he have done?" Jacob asked as he tried to pull air into his lungs so the oxygen could feed his blood. Energy. He needed it badly.

"Ask your pitiful mate." His tone held slight amusement as his dark eyes brushed over Jacob from head to toe before he turned.

Jacob rubbed his chest as he watched Taras walk away, his strides angry as he entered the club. Jacob got back onto his bike, pulled from the driveway, and headed home.

Chapter Five

Shelby was beside himself. Jacob hadn't returned. Had something happened to his mate? Had he freaked out after he left and decided never to return? The possibilities were endless, and Shelby didn't have an answer.

He ran from his bedroom and into the kitchen where the house phone was. There was no way he was going to disobey Christian again. But he could ask the prince to find Jacob for him. Just to make sure the man was all right of course.

"Prince," Shelby said as he mangled his thumbnail between his teeth, "my mate hasn't returned to me, and you know that he has a sickness inside of him. Can you please find out where he is?"

He could hear Christian sigh on the other end of the phone. "What makes you think there is something wrong, young one?"

Because my mate isn't here with me, duh.

Of course he didn't say that out loud. Even though Christian was a kind prince, he wasn't that crazy.

"He's sick, Prince. What if something bad happened to him?"

"I'll find him for you, Shelby. But you cannot go into a panic whenever he is not near."

Yes he could. It was perfectly logical behavior.

"Thank you," he said as he hung up the phone. If Jacob didn't want to see him anymore, Shelby wanted to know. It would tear him apart, but at least he would know the reason Jacob wasn't here. It was the not knowing that was driving him crazy. Bad things happened to good people. Shelby knew this. That was why he wasn't taking any chances.

* * * *

Jacob sat on his couch, grabbing the ball from Mango's mouth and tossing it back across the room. It wasn't a happy game, and Mango knew this. He didn't race after the ball excitedly. The German Shepherd just trotted across the room, retrieved the toy, and then trotted back, as if pacifying Jacob.

He sat there thinking about Taras and Shelby. He thought about how he was so damn tired all of the time, and how damn thankful he was that the little shit hadn't made him bleed. Over the past two months, bleeding was a big concern to Jacob. Sometimes it became uncontrollable to where he had to go to the hospital for help.

He tossed the ball again, only this time it slammed into the wall so hard that Mango barked and ran back over to Jacob. He hated this disease, hated feeling so damn tired and helpless. And if a donor was found for him, he would be even more helpless with recovery. What was he going to do about Shelby then?

"I don't think the wall has done anything to you."

Jacob glanced over his shoulder, having no energy to jump up and fight. It was the prince, standing by the double glass doors to the patio. He glanced over to see the doors were still closed, which meant the guy did that freaky appearing thing.

"Is there a reason you're here?" Jacob asked as he sat back, staring at the spot he had just thrown the ball. Thank goodness it had been a tennis ball. There were no cracks in the wall, but the plant took one for the team.

"I'm afraid we have not been formally introduced. My name is Christian Leanthony Espelimbergo. Shelby begged me to find you and make sure you are unharmed," the prince said as he leaned against the kitchen counter, cupping his hands together. "I see that you are unharmed."

Jacob laughed, the sound cracked and dry. "It depends on your definition of unharmed."

Christian stared at Jacob, his black eyes very serious. "You are referring to your sickness." It was a statement, not a question.

Jacob's voice lowered as he swallowed his anger down. "Yes."

Christian nodded. Jacob stared at the man's inky-black eyes, feeling as though he were falling forward, falling straight toward the prince. He blinked a few times, his mind clearing. "You can tell Shelby I'm fine." His tone was one of irritation.

"And why can't you deliver this message yourself?" the prince asked. He didn't sound pissed that Jacob had snapped at him, but Jacob could almost feel the warning in the man's steps as he moved a little closer.

To hell with it. Why hide the truth? It sucked to admit his weakness, but Jacob felt that Shelby did deserve some sort of explanation. The guy had been nothing but nice to Jacob.

"I ran into one of your vampires. He pretty much dusted me off in the parking lot. How can I defend Shelby if I can't even kick a little pipsqueak's ass?"

The prince's eyes blazed as he took another step closer. "And does this pipsqueak have a name?"

"Look," Jacob said as he stood, feeling a little wobbly. "I don't need you fighting my battles. It's bad enough I got my ass kicked. What would the neighbors think if you ran in to defend me?"

Christian's lip lifted slightly, as if he were considering a smile. "Man to man, I understand your point of view, Jacob. But vampire to human, there are things you don't know about."

"Like what?"

Christian did smile this time. It wasn't a broad smile, but his lips did lift. "A vampire defends his mate. Do you know the dishonor Shelby would feel if he knew you ran from him because you could not defend yourself? Humans were not meant to defeat vampires,"

Christian said as he slid his slim fingers into his pants pockets. "I'm just stating a fact."

"So you're saying that it's Shelby's job to defend me?" No matter how many times Jacob twisted that idea over in his mind, it just wasn't fitting. Jacob the badass biker needing a little vampire to fight his battles? "No thanks."

"Pride cometh before the fall," the prince said as he tsked. "Do you think a man's worth is measured by his physical strength?"

"Hell yeah," Jacob said without hesitation. "That's a big part of it."

"I'll never understand humans." Christian reached down and patted Mango on his head. The German Shepherd whimpered and then moved closer to Jacob. Even the damn dog knew someone more powerful than both of them combined was standing in the living room.

When the prince looked back up at Jacob, he felt a jolt of electricity shoot through him. "What did you just do to me?"

"Nothing," the prince replied. "I do apologize, though. Sometimes my powers…" Christian looked as though he were groping for the right word. Somehow Jacob knew the man had no problem expressing himself. "Fluctuate."

Fluctuate my ass. The man was doing it on purpose, trying to prove a point that vampires were stronger than humans. Christian didn't need to prove a point. Taras had been an excellent teacher earlier.

Point proven.

"You can tell Shelby yourself that you do not wish to be his mate."

Jacob choked out a half laugh. "I see what you're doing."

"Do you?" Christian asked as he stared down at Mango. Why did the vampire keep looking at his dog?

"Fine." Jacob threw his hands up in the air. "But let me feed Mango first. This might take a while."

Once Jacob made sure the level of food and water in Mango's feeding stations were satisfactory, he loaded up his meds in his travel bag. There was a flap built right into the wall next to the sliding doors, so Jacob didn't have to worry about Mango needing to go outside. The backyard was fenced in as well.

"Let's go."

Christian placed his hand on Jacob's shoulder, and within a millisecond Jacob was standing in Shelby's bedroom.

"Good luck, Jacob," Christian said a little too happily as he disappeared.

"Are you okay?" Shelby asked as he jumped up from his bed and ran to Jacob, his hands exploring Jacob's body.

Jacob squirmed. It tickled. He opened his mouth to tell Shelby he was fine when the room swooned and Jacob collapsed.

* * * *

"Has the team reported in?" Christian asked as he sat down at his desk, his eyes focused on Christo. After hearing the news that the rogue population had grown exponentially, Christian had sent in the very best to annihilate the threat to his city.

This was his damn territory, and he planned on keeping it that way. He was trying to use every option he had before using the very last option he wanted to explore.

As badly as he wanted to reunite with his brothers, unleashing them on the rogue population wasn't the answer. It would only add to the problem. Christian was beginning to think that his brothers were becoming his only option lately.

"They have. While they were able to kill a large number, I was told that there are more than we anticipated."

Christian sighed at Christo's report. He was a little surprised he hadn't heard from Maverick or Zeus, the two wolf alphas that ran the shifter packs east of his manor. Rogues tended to drift that way from time to time. And if the numbers had truly tripled, then he should have heard from the two.

"What do they need?" Christian asked.

"A miracle," Christo said under his breath.

That wasn't the answer Christian wanted to hear.

* * * *

Shelby dropped to his knees, rolling Jacob over as he shook him. "Jacob!" he shouted and then looked around the room. Shelby had no clue what he was looking for, but helplessness seized him and made it hard for him to think clearly.

His mate had passed out in front of him. Shelby knew that humans fainted sometimes. But seeing his mate drop to the floor, that knowledge didn't help. He shook Jacob again, praying out loud that the man would open his eyes.

What did Shelby know about saving a life?

He jumped to his feet, ready to race for help when he heard a barely audible moan. He spun around to see Jacob's eyelids flickering open. Getting back down onto his knees, Shelby lightly tapped Jacob on his face.

"I'm fine," Jacob said, another low moan escaping his lips.

"You are not fine," Shelby said as he leaned back, giving his human room to breathe. "You passed out. That does not qualify as fine."

As Jacob lay there, his light-brown eyes staring up at Shelby, a grin slowly formed. Shelby wasn't sure why Jacob was smiling. Nothing about this situation was funny. "Nothing about this is humorous," Shelby said in his best chastising voice. "You passed out. What part of that is funny?"

"I woke up to an angel."

"Hardly."

"It's a matter of opinion."

Shelby wasn't sure what to say. *What do you say when someone thinks you are an angel?* It was a long-fought debate whether vampires had souls or not. An ongoing debate that Shelby wasn't about to discuss with Jacob right now. "Fine, this angel wants to know why you passed out."

"Not enough oxygen is being absorbed into my already-low count of red blood cells."

Shelby repeated the sentence in his head, and then his eyes widened. "You're getting sicker, aren't you?"

"Watch out," Jacob said without answering Shelby's question as he rolled to his side and then sat up. Shelby moved away so his mate could get to his feet. He didn't like the unhealthy pallor of Jacob's skin, but Shelby was figuring the human out quickly. When Jacob didn't want to talk about something, he wasn't going to budge.

Jacob shrugged his jacket off, tossing it on the end of the bed as he sat down on the mattress. "Stop looking so worried, Shelby." Jacob reached a hand out, and Shelby instantly went to him. He should be yelling at Jacob for downplaying things. He knew his mate was making the situation seem less serious than it truly was. But seeing Jacob reach out for him, wanting him near, Shelby could do nothing but go to the man.

Shit. He was helpless around his mate. That meant no matter how mad Shelby became at Jacob, all the guy had to do was hold out his hand and Shelby would come running. *Double shit.* That wasn't going to work if Shelby was the one caring for Jacob. The human was too damn stubborn to listen to anyone.

Even if what was being said was logical.

Jacob pulled Shelby into the apex of his thighs, resting his large hands on Shelby's back, keeping him close. "Stop worrying so much about me. I'm fine."

Shelby had a hard time looking away from Jacob's soulful eyes. He could see the truth in their brown depths, but he also knew that if Jacob believed it, then the man wouldn't think he was lying.

Shelby was not convinced.

Goose bumps broke out over Shelby's body, a rush of prickling warmth as Jacob's hand slowly lowered to his ass, cupping it. Damn it, he was going to give in. Shelby shivered, as if a cool breeze had just blown by him. Jacob pulled him closer, his head leaning toward Shelby.

"Do you want me, Shelby?" His voice was a rich growl of sound as his eyes burned into Shelby's.

"Yes," he said softly. "I do."

Jacob's smile widened with pleasure as he grabbed the hem of Shelby's shirt and lifted it from his body, exposing his narrow chest. It was a different sensation than when Jacob had showered him and laid him to bed yesterday.

This seemed more intimate, more daring. He was being undressed for Jacob's pleasure, and Shelby prayed the man didn't stop.

"You're so pale," he said as his fingers touched Shelby's skin lightly. If Jacob hadn't been looking at Shelby with desire, he would have thought the statement an insult. But Jacob's eyes were filled with heat, as if a fire had been lit behind the light-brown irises.

Shelby gazed at Jacob, willing the man with his mind to finish undressing him. He wasn't glamoring the human. That would be wrong to do to one's mate. So he just stood there sending up a prayer instead.

His legs quivered, feeling as though he had been standing on them for far too long as Jacob leaned forward, his tongue slowly leaving his mouth to lap at one of Shelby's nipples. The cool air in the room brushed over the moisture, making the brown disk tighten. His legs shook some more.

Jacob kissed the nipple and then moved his head to taste the other one, the neglected one. Shelby hissed when Jacob teased the flesh with his teeth, rolling it around. His fingers curled at his sides, his cock growing in his pants as Jacob sucked the skin into his mouth.

His pulse was thudding in his throat as he tried to swallow it back down. Tiny pleasure claws were sinking in at his groin and working their way up his spine, wrapping around his chest where Jacob was enjoying Shelby's nipple.

He shifted his weight to his right foot, hoping he wasn't the one to pass out this time. It was a real possibility as Jacob's fingers dug gently into Shelby's back, drawing him closer into the nook of Jacob's thighs.

Shelby glanced down at the same time Jacob looked up, his human smiling at him from around his taut nipple. Something deep, primal snapped inside of Shelby at the boyish grin. He pulled his chest away from Jacob and kicked his pants off, freeing them from his body. Jacob leaned back on the bed, propping himself up by his elbows as he watched Shelby undress.

Deep approval swam in the depths of Jacob's eyes as Shelby moved closer, crawling up on the bed. Jacob didn't move. Only his eyes followed Shelby as he reached down and released the buckle of Jacob's belt and then pushed the two leather straps aside.

Jacob's intense stare was starting to chip away at Shelby's bravery. He averted his eyes, concentrating on unsnapping the button on Jacob's jeans. When it popped free, Shelby pinched the zipper in between his fingers and slowly drew it down. He could see the large bulge in Jacob's pants. It throbbed once, almost as if it were beckoning Shelby to reach in and free the flesh.

"It won't bite you," Jacob said, his deep baritone teasing.

No, it wouldn't. Shelby was well aware of that fact. He reached out, running his knuckles over the swollen jeans. The erection jerked again. He glanced up to see that Jacob was watching him intently.

Hooking his index finger into the waistband of Jacob's underwear, he pulled the fabric down until his fingers touched the denim of Jacob's jeans. His eyes took in the long, thick patch of hair running from Jacob's navel to his groin where it spread out like a bed of soft hair. And in that bed a cockhead was nestled, weeping clear liquid until it ran down the soft flesh and touched the bed of hair. He could see veins standing out on the shaft, one long one dipping down past the waistband and disappearing.

Shelby licked his lips as he inhaled. He could smell his mate's preseminal fluid strongly, along with the earthy scent of man. *My man.* Moving backward on his knees, Shelby gave himself enough room to lean forward and taste the clear liquid with the tip of his tongue.

Jacob's thighs tensed and then relaxed, but Shelby could feel how rigid they truly were underneath him. His tongue curled around the liquid, dragging it from the tiny slit like a bear eating honey, slowly, sighing.

He had to move out of the way when he felt Jacob push his pants further down his thighs, exposing the thick muscles of his legs and the light dusting of hair that sprinkled the lengths. Shelby ran his fingers over the wisps of hair, feeling how it tickled his hand.

Jacob's cock throbbed in his other hand as Shelby let his palm ghost over the hair, barely touching it before he glanced back up. His mate was leaning on his elbows once more, his light-brown eyes changing, darkening to almost the color of copper.

Shelby swung back around and settled between the man's thighs, dipping his head once more. Only this time he sucked the salty flesh past his lips, using his tongue as a massaging appendage as it rolled around the head and worked its way down the shaft. He could feel every bump and ridge with his tongue.

Jacob moaned and fell onto his back, his hands skating over Shelby's hair, making his scalp tingle as he breathed through his nose. Extreme pleasure was coming off of Jacob like heat on hot pavement, dancing up from Jacob's body almost visibly.

Encouraged, Shelby swallowed Jacob's length, humming as he worked the flesh deeper into his mouth.

"Yes, Shelby," Jacob said as he moaned. His thighs spread as far apart as they could with the jeans still down around Jacob's knees. He gave Shelby a little more room. Shelby angled his body until the steel-hard contour of Jacob's thigh was inserted between his legs, his balls pressing between his own skin, the flesh that felt like steel. The sparse sprinkles of hair only added to his nerve-laden flesh, sharp flares of pleasure shooting to his cock.

"I can feel your cock on my leg, baby. Ride it. Ride it, hard," Jacob said in a rough plea as his thigh pressed harder into Shelby's balls. Shelby began to move up and down Jacob's leg as he worked the hard flesh in his mouth. He was being pulled into a heated maelstrom, drowning in it as Jacob ran his hands through Shelby's hair, more roughly now.

Shelby released Jacob's cock, letting the erection slip past his moistened lips as he crawled up his mate's body, grabbing at the black T-shirt, yanking it up Jacob's broad, hard chest. He attached his lips to one perfectly shaped nipple, whimpering as he ground his balls into the firm strength of Jacob's abdomen.

Shelby's body jerked slightly when he felt Jacob reach behind him, his wet fingers rimming his hole. As his fingernails dug into Jacob's chest, he pressed his body back, testing, wanting.

He groaned as he lapped when the tip of Jacob's finger pressed inside his body. After sliding his hand under the pillow, Shelby laid the bottle of lube onto Jacob's chest, never looking up at his mate.

He heard the cap snick, and seconds later the pressure was back at his entrance. It was more than one finger, the increased pressure telling him so. Shelby nursed at Jacob's chest as he closed his eyes, letting go of a rough, hard breath as a shudder ran the course of his body.

"Lift your hips, Shelby," Jacob said as he tapped Shelby's hip bone with his free hand.

Shelby released Jacob's nipple as he canted his hips, raising them as he felt the blunt tip of Jacob's cock probing at his stretched hole.

"Now lower yourself. Take your time, just what you can take."

Shelby nodded as he slid to his knees, taking Jacob's dick into his ass by small, measured increments. Jacob circled his fingers around Shelby's jaw, turning his head until Shelby was staring down into coppery pools. Jacob watched Shelby's face as his body slowly lowered. His eyes fluttered, and his lips parted slightly, his breathing a little less steady.

"You're stunningly handsome, Shelby," Jacob said as he ran the pad of his thumb over Shelby's bottom lip. "So damn gorgeous."

Shelby managed a wavering smile as he finally ran out of shaft and sat back.

"And so fucking unbelievably tight." Jacob's fingers curled around Shelby's hips, encouraging him to move. Shelby placed his hands on Jacob's biceps and pulled forward. As he began to sit back, Jacob's pelvis came crashing forward, their bodies colliding and sending erotic sensations crashing through Shelby's body.

All Shelby could do was hold on as Jacob began to thrust his cock up into Shelby's ass. He licked his lips, his eyes focusing on the beating pulse in Jacob's neck. It was straining, the corded muscles twitching as Jacob made love to him.

Shelby leaned forward and licked a long path from Jacob's collarbone to his ear. "Can I bite you?" he asked around the shell of his mate's ear.

"Yes." Jacob ground out the word.

Shelby felt his teeth ache, his mouth water, but fear gripped him. His mate was sick, weak. He knew he had to drink from Jacob in order to bind them together, but would it hurt the human?

He decided in that second to only take enough to bind them. He always had the crimson to drink to sustain him. As long as his mate suffered his illness, Shelby wouldn't drink from him. Jacob needed all the blood he had, and then some.

Scraping his teeth along Jacob's skin, his mate shivered and then stilled. Shelby knew Jacob was waiting for the bite, for the breaking of skin. Shelby sank his teeth in, taking in Jacob's preciously low blood, feeling it splash across his tongue. He could taste the sickness. It was foul tasting, but Shelby swallowed nonetheless. It hadn't been this bad yesterday. Shelby knew his mate was getting worse, whether Jacob cared to admit this fact or not.

Jacob jerked below him, his body convulsing as his hips began to snap furiously forward, fucking Shelby hard as he cried out, his muscles locking around Shelby's body. Shelby quickly closed the wound he had inflicted and then leaned back, grabbing his cock and stroking it twice before he was crying out, ropes of white seed spurting out onto Jacob's chest.

Jacob stilled once again. Shelby glanced down, fear wrapping around his spine that his mate had passed out once more. Jacob was lying there smiling up at him, his eyes pools of satiation as he brushed Shelby's sweat-soaked hair from his eyes.

"My little vampire."

Shelby grinned as he pressed his cheek into the palm of Jacob's hand. They were mated now. Jacob should live as long as Shelby did. But there was one large fissure racing up the seam of Shelby's plan.

His mate still smelled sick.

Chapter Six

Shelby moved around Jacob's body, knowing it intimately now as the music washed over them. Christian had lifted his restriction, allowing Shelby to come back to the club. But the prince had also told him that he better not disobey again.

Shelby wasn't crazy. When the prince gave an order, any sane person tended to listen. Which only made him question his sanity for going against the original vampire the first time. Shelby smiled when he saw Eli bringing him a glass of ice water. Jersey's mate handed the cold glass to him before disappearing back through the crowd.

"Here," Shelby said as he lifted the glass to Jacob.

"Thank you," Jacob said as he took the glass and drank the water down in just a few gulps. Was that normal? He could see the beads of sweat lining Jacob's dark brows and began to worry.

His gut told him this wasn't right.

"We can rest," Shelby said as he plucked the glass from Jacob's hand.

His mate shook his head, a grin lighting up his face. "I'm fine."

Shelby was getting really tired of those two words. All vampires knew that taking care of their mate was top priority. They didn't get another. It was crazy to abuse one's mate, but Shelby had seen it happen before. Who would want to spend eternity cowering at someone's feet? And who would want to spend eternity making someone cower? It was useless energy in Shelby's opinion.

"You have to rest, mate."

"I said I'm fine," Jacob said as a red flush crept up into his neck. The man was angry. Shelby knew Jacob didn't want to be coddled, but his health was at stake here and he wasn't taking any chances. The man would just have to be spitting mad. Deciding that arguing his point wasn't going to get him far, Shelby threaded through the crowd toward the bar.

If Jacob continued to dance without Shelby, he would drag his mate away from the dancing humans and vampires. Shelby sat the glass on the counter and turned to see Jacob emerging from the wall of dancers. He was softly frowning as he headed toward Shelby.

Shelby took a step forward. Jacob wasn't frowning because he was mad. No, he was frowning because something was wrong. Even with the entire club filled with people, he could feel Jacob's fear. It grabbed at him like a slick, black ooze with painfully sharp claws.

He raced toward his mate as Jacob paled and then swooned. Shelby caught the tall, muscular man and pulled him along until he reached the prince's office and then kicked the door open.

The prince immediately stood. Shelby glimpsed at the men sitting around the table, but he quickly ignored them as he sat his mate on the couch. Jacob closed his eyes and slumped back into the leather.

"He's dying!" Shelby cried as he ran to the prince. "Save him, convert him, please."

Christian walked over to Jacob and squatted in front of the man, his dark eyes studying Shelby's mate. "He is growing weaker, young one."

"Then convert him," Shelby said in panic. What was so complicated about his request? Only Christian, along with Nija and the elders, had the power to convert a human into a vampire. It saved the vampire population from exploding, but it made converting Jacob a lot harder since Shelby didn't have that power. He had to rely on the prince to help him out.

"He will recover, Shelby," Christian said as he stood. Shelby balled his fists up at his side, reminding himself who he was standing in front of. It wouldn't do him any good to lose his temper.

"But he is still dying," Shelby pointed out.

"Yes, Shelby, he is. But the decision for Jacob to be converted is Jacob's alone. He must be the one who wants this." Christian gazed down at Shelby, his expression one of sympathy. "I will not force a conversion on anyone who does not wish it."

"But you've converted men before without their consent. Look at Eli," Shelby pointed out harshly. He could see by Christian's face that he was pushing, but then again, Shelby was fighting for his mate's life.

"That is different. Eli didn't have a voice to give his consent. Your mate will wake. Ask him what he wants, Shelby. The choice is his. Don't take that away from him." Christian turned toward the men sitting at the table. All eyes were on Shelby. "I think we can pick this meeting up later." Christian waved for the men to leave the room.

Shelby turned back toward Jacob, his mate's eyes still closed. Once he heard the last man leave the room, Shelby crawled onto the couch, sitting next to his mate.

"No, Shelby," Jacob said weakly. "That's cheating death." Jacob licked his lips. "Everyone has their time on earth and their time to die. Why should I be any different?"

"Because you are my mate," Shelby said softly, tears springing in his eyes. "Because I love you, Jacob Marshall."

Jacob grinned as he slowly opened his eyes, touching Shelby's face with his hand. "I still have time. The doctors will find a bone marrow donor that will match."

"But that's cheating as well," Shelby said and then felt an urge to kick himself. He didn't want his mate opting out of that option as well. "If you are converted, you will never get sick again."

Jacob's eyes saddened as he stared at Shelby. "No, my little vampire."

Shelby choked on his tears as he leaned forward, wrapping his arms around Jacob's strong frame. "I'm scared, Jacob. I can't lose you."

"I'm scared too, Shelby. But everyone has their time."

Shelby wanted to argue. He wanted to force the conversion on the stubborn human, but he knew that it was wrong. In his heart, he knew he could never force Jacob to do anything, even live.

"Hey." Jacob grabbed Shelby's arm and shook it lightly. "I'm not going anywhere, okay?"

Shelby nodded, even though he knew Jacob's statement was a lie. He knew that no matter what Christian, the coven, or even Jacob himself said, Shelby was going to lose his mate.

It was only a matter of when.

* * * *

Jacob chuckled as Shelby stared strangely at his motorcycle. The little vampire looked lost, as if he had never seen a bike before. His helmet sat sideways on his head, the strap dangling loosely. "You want me to ride this?"

"With me," Jacob said as he placed his own black helmet with blazing fire down the sides on his head. "It's not complicated. I'll do all the work. All you have to do is hold on to me."

Shelby nodded, the loose strap swaying around, but the man still didn't looked convinced. Jacob knew that if he didn't get Shelby onto his bike, there was a large possibility that his mate would go running back into the club.

Jacob had been waiting to take Shelby out. Once Christian had given his permission—and that still rankled Jacob that he had to ask for it—Jacob knew what he wanted to do with the man.

"But we are sitting on gasoline. It combusts," Shelby pointed out.

Jacob reached across the bike and hooked the strap under Shelby's chin. "That's not going to happen, babe."

"But it could," Shelby argued.

"Can we go, or are we going to debate about this until sunrise?"

Shelby looked like he wanted to debate about it. Jacob slid his leg over the bike. "Get behind me, sweetheart."

Shelby let out an audible sigh, letting Jacob know he wasn't with this plan. Jacob grinned as the short vampire climbed onto the back of his bike. He turned the key. The bike roared to life. His hand quickly shot behind him and stopped Shelby from jumping off. "You're safe."

"If you say so."

Jacob drove from the parking lot at a slow rate…until he hit the street. He could feel Shelby's fingers digging into his sides as he drove down the city street. He was only going the speed limit, but apparently even that was too fast for the vamp.

As they rode along, Jacob could feel Shelby's fingers loosening slightly, his body more relaxed as Shelby leaned closer into Jacob. He was half tempted to get onto the expressway, but he didn't want to peel Shelby from the ground.

The man was sure to jump ship at the higher rate of speed.

Jacob enjoyed the night more than the day. There was just something alluring about the darkness that always made him want to be out in the streets at night, either hanging with associates or by himself. The autumn air blew across his face, his glasses sitting snugly against his eyes. The streets were lit up, the night thriving.

The bike thrummed between his thighs as Jacob pulled into his driveway. He could hear Mango barking, telling Jacob he knew his master was home. He shut the bike off and removed his helmet, hanging his glasses on the handlebars of his bike. Shelby climbed from behind him, his legs wobbling slightly.

"That was fun," Shelby admitted as he took off his helmet and glasses, setting the pair on the soft leather seat of the bike. The man looked like he meant it.

Jacob showed Shelby into his home, Mango running to greet them at the door.

Shelby shrieked.

"He's not going to hurt you, Shelby. Mango is a good dog."

For the second time tonight, Shelby didn't look convinced. Mango shoved his nose into Shelby, sniffing him as if he were searching for something—or trying to decide if Shelby was safe enough for his master. Shelby stood there, spine straight, as he allowed Mango his inspection.

Mango barked his approval as he sat back on his haunches, his tongue hanging out of the side of his mouth as his tail swished back and forth.

"I told you he was a good boy."

"I–I like dogs," Shelby said as he stayed tucked behind Jacob.

"You do?"

"Well, Mango is the first dog I've met, but he does seem nice, even though he has very sharp teeth."

"So do you," Jacob said, a humorous inflection in his tone. Shelby glared at Jacob, but there was no heat behind the expression. He walked into the kitchen as Shelby took a seat on the couch. Mango decided he liked Shelby better tonight and followed him, sitting right in front of the man and then lying down at his feet.

Jacob chuckled softly at the stiff way Shelby was sitting as he grabbed his medication and a bottled water from the refrigerator. Once he downed the meds, he dropped down next to Shelby. "You don't get out much, do you?"

Shelby shook his head, his eyes trained on Mango. "Not really. There are rogues out there, and I'm not very good at fighting them."

"Rogues?" Why didn't Jacob like the sound of that? What he liked even less was the idea of Shelby having to defend himself against whatever a rogue was.

"They are vampires that gave in to bloodlust. They drink until their victim is bone-dry, leaving their victim dead. They don't have any compassion or reasoning. They can talk, respond, and figure out inconsequential problems, but their humanity is gone, drowned beneath the overwhelming need for blood."

Gee, didn't that sound just peachy. Jacob had never run into a rogue. He probably wouldn't be sitting here right now if he had. From what Shelby described, the creatures must be pretty damn strong.

"And Christian allows them to run free?" Somehow Jacob knew Christian was in charge of more than just the club. The man gave off a vibe that screamed master vampire.

His eyes alone had pulled Jacob in, making him feel as though he would do whatever the man asked. And that just pissed him off to no end.

"He's trying to take care of the problem," Shelby said as he tucked his feet closer to the couch, away from Mango. From what Jacob was hearing, Mango was the least of his problems. There were vampires running around draining humans completely dry.

Shit.

"He's called in the best from each coven, sending the vampires out in search of the rogues," Shelby said.

Vampires hunting vampires. Somehow the two didn't go hand in hand in Jacob's mind. It was like sending good cops out to kill bad cops. Okay, not a very good analogy. "I think I've digested enough for one night." He really didn't want to hear any more. The news that rogue vampires were out there killing humans was already going to give him nightmares.

Mango's head lifted from the floor, a low warning growl rumbling from his chest. He was looking directly at the sliding glass doors. Jacob leaned forward to get a better look, and so did Shelby. Mango got up, barking as he began to back away.

Jacob had never seen Mango back away. He was a German Shepherd after all. That breed was built to protect. Jacob jumped from the couch as the glass shattered, large and small pieces of glass flying everywhere. He turned, pulling Shelby into his chest as he tried to shield the small man from the flying missiles.

"Oh crap," Shelby said nervously as he looked at the man standing in Jacob's kitchen, his eyes black with a circle of bloodred rimming them. "That's the man who attacked me!"

"Rogue?"

Shelby nodded. Jacob wasn't sure how to fight the thing off. He didn't have any weapons in his home. Even if he did, he wasn't sure a gun would stop the creature.

"Hang on," Shelby shouted as the rogue raced toward them. Shelby grabbed Jacob's arm and then reached down to grab the scruff of Mango's neck as they disappeared from Jacob's house, ending up in Shelby's bedroom.

Damn if that little trick didn't come in handy.

His heart was slamming in his chest, the adrenaline making Jacob slightly dizzy as he sat down on the bed. "How do you kill those things?" Not that he was planning on launching a crusade to hunt them down or anything.

"Take out their hearts."

Figures.

"Sunlight?"

Shelby shook his head.

Damn.

"Crosses?"

Shelby shook his head again.

Double damn. Stake through the heart. Just great.

Mango barked as he swept through Shelby's bedroom, sticking his damn nose into everything. The dog acted like this was the first time he had been somewhere else besides Jacob's house.

"I think he likes it here. Either that or he is about to pee on my belongings," Shelby said as he stepped away from his bed, bracing himself as Mango approached and shoved his head into Shelby's leg.

"I think you're right."

"He's a good rogue detector," Shelby said as he tentatively reached out and scratched the dog's head. Mango ate it up. "We have food in the kitchen if he's hungry."

Jacob nodded as he tried to bring his racing heart back under control. Having a killer vampire crashing through his fucking sliding door wasn't exactly the perfect condition to keep his heart beating at a normal rate.

The damn thing was scary.

Maybe he should start carrying a damn gun, or a flamethrower. He wasn't sure human weapons would work against a creature like that. Jacob ran his hand over his face, knowing he couldn't go back to his place.

They were targeted. Shelby recognized the thing. It had purposefully come after Shelby.

Jacob glanced down at his hands, wondering how he would protect Shelby even if they went back to his place. He couldn't even beat one small vampire, and the one that had crashed his little party was twice the size of Taras.

"I know it's a lot to take in," Shelby said as he stepped closer to Jacob like someone afraid the freaked-out man would freak out. "But we're safe here."

"Just exactly what is this place?" He knew Shelby lived here, and this was his bedroom. Beyond that he hadn't a clue.

"My home," Shelby answered. "My coven's home."

Coven. Which meant a whole assortment of vampires slept here. "How do you know one of your coven members won't go rogue and come back here before anyone is the wiser? That thing could wipe us all out in our sleep." It was a possibility, one that was weighing heavily on Jacob's mind.

"Because Christian would know right away. He can detect them." Shelby pointed at Mango. "And we have a rogue alert dog, too."

As shaken up as he was, Jacob smiled. Mango was the best. "Don't you think you should tell Christian what happened?"

Shelby nodded, his usually perfectly combed hair bouncing until it fell over his forehead and eyes. "As soon as he comes back. If it's all the same to you, I'd rather stay in tonight."

* * * *

Christian sat at the long table in his office. Christo, Isla, and Emilio sat at the table with him. He stared down at the other end of the well-polished table at the three shifters. Maverick, the alpha of the timber wolves, had sent one of the shifters. Zeus, the alpha of the grey wolves, had sent him the other two.

The shifters sitting at the end of the table didn't belong to any pack according to the alphas, but they couldn't give him their one hundred percent guarantee since these wolf shifters weren't a part of their packs.

They sat there casually as if they weren't sitting in a club full of vampires, but a coffee shop or something like that instead. Well, at least these men had iron balls. That was a plus for Christian.

"Your duties will be to guard my coven when we sleep during the day. I am told that the alphas who sent you gentlemen have informed you of the vampire hunters?" Christian had known about the humans who hunted vampires, but he never had concrete evidence. He had it now since the hunters had planned to storm the manor during the day.

The only thing that had botched their plans was Connor, Vaughn's mate. They had kidnapped the human instead, using him to lure Vaughn into an ambush for some sort of revenge. If it weren't for Connor, they just may have succeeded.

Killing Christian wouldn't be easy. Most humans thought that vampires fell into a deep, coma-like sleep during the daylight hours. Not true. They could get up and walk around freely inside the manor. They just couldn't go outside.

The largest of the three nodded. "We were informed."

"And you are aware that myself and my coven are not helpless during daylight hours?" Christian was making this known up front just in case one of the shifters had any ideas. He didn't know them after all.

The one sitting off to the left gave a slight grin and then covered his mouth as if he were resting his arm as he nodded. The other two hid their surprise expertly.

"Then you shall start in the morning."

The three shifters stood, and Christian could see the wariness in the vampires' eyes as his coven members assessed the shifters. He knew this decision wasn't going to be an easy adjustment, but they had no choice. If the hunters attacked during the day, Christian could only imagine the chaos that would rain down on his coven.

He was the oldest, the master, the original, but he didn't want to take any chances on the loss of life that would take place as he took down the hunters one by one.

There would be no way he would be able to protect every single vampire and fight the hunters as well.

He watched the shifters give him one last look before they left his office. The one that had known that vampires could walk during sunlight hours glanced back at the men sitting around the table, an excited gleam in his eyes. Christian was going to have a private talk with that particular shifter. Because he wasn't sure if that look was the thrill of killing the hunters, or the vampires.

Chapter Seven

Mango stared up at Christian, his head cocked sideways as if studying the prince. Shelby fidgeted. He wasn't sure how Christian would take the dog being at the coven, but he had grown to like the German Shepherd.

"You say he alerted you to a rogue's presence before the vampire attacked your home?" Christian asked as he glanced down at Mango. A grin was trying to form on Shelby's lips, but he repressed it. The prince of vampires and the dog seemed to be considering each other.

Shelby didn't want the odds in Mango's favor dropping.

"Yes, Christian. He gave a low growl and then barked right before the creature attacked," Jacob said as he glanced between both creatures staring each other down.

"What of his…needs?" Christian asked.

"I can make sure they are taken care of. I've been taking care of his needs since I brought him home," Jacob answered. Shelby could tell Jacob was very overprotective of the dog from the inflection in his tone. It had become gentle when he glanced down at Mango. "He's a good dog, Christian." His words were spoken with a conviction.

"Very well," Christian said as he gave a slight nod. "But if he tears anything up or leaves little gifts lying about, I'm holding you responsible, Jacob." Christian waved a hand at the dog, his face still reserved. "I'm not sure if it was just a fluke or if he can really detect rogues."

Shelby wanted to pump his arms in triumph, but bit the smile back. He knew, as well as Jacob, that his mate couldn't go home again, not anytime soon. So having Christian approve Mango was important.

If Christian had said that Mango couldn't stay, he knew Jacob would have taken Mango and left. It wasn't a chance Shelby wanted to take. He was praying Christian said yes or things would have gotten tricky. Shelby wasn't going to allow his mate to leave without him, and Shelby would most definitely have followed the human.

The problem would have been that pesky sun. Becoming crispy fried wasn't his idea of a good time. When Christian left the bedroom, Shelby grinned widely at Jacob. "I told you he would say yes."

"You were sweating bullets. Admit it," Jacob replied as he tapped the end of Shelby's nose with his finger. "I could see the sheen of sweat gathering over your brows."

"Vampires don't sweat," Shelby harrumphed and then grinned. "But I was a bit tense." He patted Mango on the head, surprised with himself how quickly he adjusted to the large dog. When he first spotted the German Shepherd coming his way in Jacob's home, he thought he was going to wet himself.

Thank goodness it hadn't come to that.

"I need to get him some food and bowls. He needs his toys as well," Jacob said as he patted Mango's shank. The dog wagged his tail as he looked up at Jacob like he was the cheese on his crackers.

"That'll have to wait until sunset. Dawn is too close. Can he eat leftovers?"

Jacob looked surprised. "What kind of leftovers are in a vampire's home?"

"Jersey and Buck eat human food, as well as Connor. I can rummage in the fridge for something Mango will like." Shelby looked down at the dog. "What does he like?"

Jacob chuckled. "Anything."

Shelby watched as the shutters to his windows slowly began to lower, indicating that dawn was coming soon. The sound of metal folding down into place was loud in his bedroom. Jacob glanced up,

watching as the grinding metal slid until the outside could no longer
be seen.

"I'll be right back," Shelby said as he patted Mango on the head
and then left his bedroom, seeking out Christian. He had questions,
and he knew only the prince had the answers. He found the man in the
hallway carrying his son high on his shoulders as he patted the baby
vampire's back.

Minzhe cried gently over the prince's shoulder as Christian paced
up and down the hallway. The only time Shelby saw Christian come
out of the bedroom with the baby was when he was trying not to wake
his mates.

"Is there something you need, young one?" Christian asked as he
settled the child into his arms and then fed the baby his wrist. It was
normal to feed a baby vampire this way. They needed their
nourishment after all. Shelby knew that the more Minzhe drank, the
quicker he would grow. Baby vampires developed at a faster rate than
human babies. When Minzhe was six months old, he would look like
a two-year-old human toddler.

"I wanted to ask you something about Jacob."

"Go ahead."

"You know that he is sick, right."

"I am aware of this," Christian said, his dark eyes studying
Shelby. "And you want to know why he is still sick even after mating
him?"

Shelby always shuddered when Christian did that. The vampire
was extremely accurate and eerily on point. "Yes."

Christian adjusted the babe in his arms. Small suckling sounds
could be heard in the hallway. "He came to you sick, Shelby. Mating
him will not cure him of this. Only conversion will. A human can live
as long as his mate when being claimed, as long as he is healthy.
Jacob is not."

He hated when the prince stated things so matter-of-factly. He
knew that Christian wasn't trying to be coldhearted, but damn if the

man didn't sound like just that. Shelby felt his chest grow heavy. Jacob had refused to be converted, and he wasn't sure he could change the man's mind.

"Is there anything I can do?"

"No."

Shelby could feel his throat constrict as he watched Minzhe feed. He felt the unfairness in all of this, the injustice that he had finally found his mate only to have that bond threatened with a human disease, a sickness that he was powerless to do anything about. The need to go to his room and force Jacob into a conversion was strong, but he knew his mate would resent him for eternity.

And that was a very long damn time to have someone mad at him.

"Talk to him, Shelby. Explain to him fully what a mate is and what being a vampire entails. He just may change his mind."

"I have talked to him," Shelby said. "He won't listen to me. He says that everyone has their time and he isn't going to cheat death." Saying the words out loud made Shelby angry. He loved Jacob. He wanted forever with the stubborn man, and they had a chance to have just that, if only his mate would say yes to being changed into a vampire.

"Then I'm afraid there is nothing either of us can do," Christian said, his voice softer as he spoke. "As harsh and cruel as my words sound, you must accept his decision and enjoy the time you do have with him."

The knowledge that Shelby was going to lose the big, badass biker was like a cold, steel spike being shoved into his heart. The agonizing loneliness that he would soon feel was already starting to fill his body.

He was to live for all eternity, unless someone killed him, and he was going to be alone. He wanted to hate Jacob for being so selfish, for condemning him to a life of merely existing, but he knew the man had a right to choose, even if he didn't choose Shelby.

Feeling defeated and broken, Shelby walked away from the prince and babe. He had no right to force what he wanted on the human.

"Shelby."

He turned to look the prince.

"He still has time to choose. Give him a reason to want to live."

Shelby nodded and then disappeared around the corner, watching his feet scuffle along as he headed back toward his bedroom. He had worried about being the perfect mate when he first discovered who Jacob was. He had fretted over not being good enough for the man. He laughed cynically to himself as he walked. Apparently he had worried for nothing. Jacob wasn't going to be around long enough for Shelby to figure out what kind of a man attracted Jacob.

And the fucked-up thought he had was that Shelby apparently wasn't Jacob's type. Not if Jacob was unwilling to stay with him.

Shelby let out a deep sigh as he opened his bedroom door to see Jacob playing with Mango. As badly as he wanted to resent his mate, it just wasn't in him to do so. The only feeling that sprang forth as he watched the dog try and tear the shirt away from Jacob's hands was pure and unrestricted love.

* * * *

Logan walked the perimeter of the manor, feeling the sun smack his back like a hot metal hand. Sweat trickled down his back and clung to his skin like a sheer wet bodysuit as he watched the grounds for intruders.

The only reason he had taken this job was because it paid so well. The money was needed, but so was a place to rest after wandering for so long. The only reason he hadn't joined a pack was because Logan hated the hierarchy of alphas and betas and so on. He liked doing things his way, on his terms.

He pulled the tee away from his chest, feeling the hot air quickly brush over his skin. It was autumn, but the days were still very hot. He headed for the shade as his eyes swept the area. Logan wasn't sure how long he would keep this gig. Pacing around a house all day wasn't very appealing to him.

But the money had been.

Christian hadn't given a specific time frame or had him sign a contract, so he knew he was free to go anytime. He didn't much care for the idea of babysitting vampires, but this job paid better than any other he had held.

He nodded at one of the other shifters the vampire had hired. He didn't trust them. The blond's eyes put Logan on edge. There was something about those small, calculating blue eyes that made Logan's hairs stand on edge. The man had been a little too smug and condescending when they had left the club before parting ways.

The blond had made it quite clear to Logan and the other shifter, what was his name again? It didn't matter. The blond had made it quite clear that he didn't like vampires, but he wanted to get paid nonetheless.

Logan had been employed before by people he didn't care for, but the blond didn't dislike vampires, he downright loathed them. So now Logan not only watched the surrounding grounds for vampire hunters and rogues, but he also watched the blond shifter as well.

His job was to protect the coven of vampires, and letting the hate-filled shifter kill the head vampire meant Logan wouldn't get paid. Logan had no doubt that the shifter wanted to do just that.

He brushed his hair from his face, feeling the sting of sweat as it dripped down into his eyes. A breeze floated lightly through the trees, rustling the leaves, but never made it down toward him.

Logan stiffened when he smelled humans on the air. Would they really attack his first day on the job? God, he hoped so. It would break up the monotony of just walking around in a damn circle.

Circling back around, Logan caught movement in the trees that lined the back property of the manor. Yippee, the fun was about to begin.

* * * *

"What's wrong?" Jacob asked as Mango began to bark. It was a hard, sharp noise that said something was wrong. It was the same bark Mango had used when that smelly thing had crashed into Jacob's sliding glass doors.

The door flew open, and Jacob immediately stood between the door and Shelby. His little vampire was asleep on the bed, helpless to defend himself. Jacob relaxed when he saw that it was Christian.

"Why is he making such a racket?" Christian asked as he waved toward Mango, who was still barking. When Christian moved further into the room, Mango took off, running straight for the hallway.

"It has to be an intruder," Jacob said as he ran after the German Shepherd. He could feel Christian following close behind as he climbed the stairs to the house above them. There was a heavy steel door at the top of the stairs. Jacob pushed it open with his shoulder, letting Mango guide the way once the door opened.

"An intruder?" Christian asked as he walked into the upstairs with Jacob. "We have shifters guarding the grounds. Logan would have radioed me if something was wrong."

Jacob shrugged as Mango ran to one of the windows in the dining room, leaping up and resting his front paws on the sill, still barking.

"I'm not sure what a damn shifter is, but Mango senses someone. You might want to get your"—he was going to say gun, but then he remembered who was behind him—"fangs out."

The prince's finely arched brow rose as a smile pulled at his lips. "My fangs?"

Jacob shrugged as he pulled the heavy drape aside and looked outside. He patted Mango's head as he searched the area with his eyes. Thoughts of Shelby being endangered clawed at his gut when he spotted a man creeping between the trees along the driveway, a gun in his hand.

If the man hadn't been armed, Jacob would have opened the front door and let Mango play fetch with the intruder's balls. The guy couldn't be a vampire rogue. It was daylight out, so this had to be a human.

Maybe.

He wasn't too sure what the hell walked the earth anymore. "What's a shifter?"

"A man that can change into an animal."

Jacob really didn't want to hear that tidbit of info. He shouldn't have asked. "Well, there's a man creeping closer to the house."

Christian was immediately beside him, hissing when he spotted the intruder getting closer. "Where in the hell are the shifters I hired?"

"Probably playing fetch in the backyard. What do you want to do about this guy?" He knew he didn't have the strength to fight with his illness, but shooting the man seemed like a damn fine idea to Jacob.

"Let him come closer," Christian said angrily. "If he is foolish enough to come inside my home, he will deserve what I do to him."

"Bloodthirsty?" Jacob asked as he pulled Mango away from the window and quieted the dog down by rubbing his hand under Mango's muzzle.

"My coven sleeps a floor below us. My mates and my son are here. I will kill anyone who threatens them."

Jacob felt the same way about Shelby, but there was pure death in Christian's dark, inky eyes. Jacob shivered at the thought of ever pissing this guy off. He looked like he could tear someone's throat out with just one hand.

And Jacob thought he was a badass? Christian trumped him and then some.

Jacob whispered to Mango to be quiet as the front door handle jiggled. The guy breaking in was ballsy as hell to use the front door, and not too damn smart either. He just hoped it wasn't one of those shifters Christian talked about and the guy changed into a damn grizzly bear or something large like that.

"He is human," Christian said as the edge of his lip lifted.

"Good to know." How in the hell did the prince do that? Jacob had been drawn to the night, to the dark side of things, his entire life, but now that he was a part of it, he was starting to question his curiosity of the unknown.

When the door cracked open, Christian was at the man's side, tearing into his throat before Jacob could even blink. The vampire had moved so quickly, so quietly that Jacob hadn't even seen him move. One minute he was standing beside Jacob, the next he was across the room and killing the intruder.

Damn.

Mango barked and Jacob just barely grabbed his collar before his dog ran to join in on the fight. German Shepherds were very good watchdogs, and would protect his family fiercely, but Jacob was quite sure Christian had this under control.

The sight made his stomach roll. There was so much damn blood. When Christian dropped the body, blood covered the front of the stranger as if someone had thrown an open one-gallon can of red paint all over him. His throat was torn, blood still pouring out of the large, gaping hole Christian had inflicted.

The prince didn't look any better himself. The thick blood covered his mouth and ran down his neck and shirt as he picked the man up and threw him back outside the door. Jacob was standing there, frozen, unsure of what he was really seeing. He wasn't afraid, which amazed him, but he wasn't moving either.

Christian glanced his way, his eyes crimson and his fangs long and sharp as hell, almost resting against his chin. Jacob looked away. What was there to say? Instead, he looked out of the window and saw someone picking the dead body up and taking it around the side of the house, toward the back.

That must have been one of the shifters.

"Does my appearance frighten you, Jacob?"

"Yes," he admitted. There was no reason to lie. The vampire would probably know if he lied anyway.

"Enough for you to leave Shelby?"

"No," he answered without hesitation. Jacob didn't think there was anything scary enough for him to leave his little vampire. But after witnessing what the man in front of him had just done, Jacob just had a big dose of reality.

Could he live in this world where there were vampires, good and bad, and some who hovered in the grey area? Could he deal with the fact that there were people right outside who could change into animals?

His hand ran over Mango's soft fur as he concentrated on the front lawn, refusing to look back over at the bloody vampire. It was bad enough the thick, coppery scent clung to the air around him, making him feel as though he were going to be sick.

"Will I be like you if I'm converted?" Jacob wasn't sure why he asked the question. Maybe there was a deep place inside of him that was considering the possibility of cheating death and living forever, or maybe he was just confirming why he didn't want to be converted at all.

"No," Christian answered. "Although there is a possibility you will have to become…" Christian paused, making Jacob turn his head. Why did he turn his head? *Damn.* The blood was still there, clinging to the vampire in a grim reminder of what had just taken place. "Physical to keep Shelby safe," he finished.

Could he tear someone's throat out to keep Shelby safe? Jacob thought about Taras and wondered if he could do something like that. The need to protect the vampire who had stolen his heart was great, but could he tear a man's flesh from his body?

Killing wasn't a question. Jacob had to do that a time or two when it had come down to him or the other guy. It was the thought of using fangs that made him pause.

"There are some things in life that a man would do to keep the one he loves safe, happy. Are you man enough, Jacob?"

Somehow he knew the prince was talking about Jacob being converted. He turned away, looking once again out of the window to the deep green grass and shrubbery that the sun was bathing in warmth. "Is it safe to go outside?"

"I believe so."

Jacob grabbed Mango's collar and walked past Christian, refusing to look the man's way as he stepped outside into the clean air. He took in a deep lungful as he gazed around. Christian had struck a sore spot inside of Jacob, and the man knew it. He had been thinking of nothing but the possibility of being converted ever since he had heard Shelby and Christian talk about it in the prince's office.

Was he man enough? Was it even a question of being man enough? He walked down the driveway, Mango at his side, keeping quiet, but staying right next to him.

Jacob hadn't been a saint in his lifetime and never claimed to be one. But he had tried to live by some sort of moral code. He knew Christian was only defending his home and family when the intruder came through the door, but the sight of all that blood kept flashing in front of Jacob's eyes.

He wasn't sure why, but seeing that blood only reminded Jacob how very few red blood cells he carried within him. He knew he wanted more time with Shelby, more time to explore what they could have between them, but he also knew that there could be a very good chance that a donor wouldn't be found for him.

Not only did he have a rare blood disorder, he was also fucking lucky enough to have a rare blood type.

Talk about fate fucking him over royally.

Yay for him.

Chapter Eight

Jacob rested his arm on the wall above his head as he leaned his forehead against the cool drywall. He had just talked with his doctor and was told no donor had been found yet, but he was getting sicker. It was hard to even get up in the evenings now.

Not only was he tiring very quickly these days, but the doctor warned him about infections. He was more susceptible to them now since his white blood cells were so low.

Jacob straightened and then pulled his shirt back over his head. The doc had given him more prescriptions. He was sick and tired of prescriptions. He wanted to be cured, or at the very least, med-free.

Opening the exam room door, Jacob walked outside where Logan was waiting for him. Christian had insisted Logan drive him in. Maybe the guy was afraid Jacob would pass out behind the wheel or something. There was a good possibility these days.

They drove back in silence, which Jacob was grateful for. Once they arrived back at the manor, Jacob walked down the steps, going to Shelby's room. The small vampire wasn't asleep. He was sitting up waiting, his eyes anxious.

"What did he say?"

Jacob was amazed Shelby hadn't browbeaten him into being converted. The man had accepted Jacob's decision and hadn't argued, but he could see the dull sadness in Shelby's eyes every time Jacob had to sit and rest. It was affecting not only Jacob, but Shelby as well.

Was he really being selfish by denying himself the chance to be cured? But being cured resulted in being converted.

"Not good," he admitted honestly. "They still haven't found a donor for me yet." He didn't bother to tell Shelby that even if a donor was found, he had been informed that he wasn't at the top of the list. Jacob had never asked how a conversion took place and wondered briefly if he had to die to be reborn.

That would suck.

Shelby nodded at Jacob's news and then glanced down at his hands, picking at his fingernails. "Did they say how long?"

How long until I die. He knew Shelby wasn't going to say the word *die.* No one liked asking someone how long they had until they dropped dead. "He's not sure, but he says I'm getting worse."

He saw Shelby's chest contract and knew the vampire had taken in a quick burst of breath. Jacob crossed the room and sat on the bed next to Shelby. He grabbed the small man's hands, stopping him from picking his nails completely off. Nothing was said between them.

Jacob stood, undressing. Shelby glanced up at him from under his lashes, watching Jacob intently, but staying seated. Jacob tossed his clothes aside as he crawled up onto the bed and lay back. "Come here, Shelby."

Shelby shook his head. "You're too weak."

"Too weak for sex?" Jacob asked. "Never."

A smile played lightly on Shelby's lips as he turned, crawling up into Jacob's arms. He wore a pair of plaid cotton pajama bottoms. They kind of looked sexy on the slim man's frame. The colors ranged from honey yellow to maroon. Jacob slid his hands into the waistband, playing with the stretchy band that surrounded Shelby's waist, but didn't push them down the vampire's body.

Shelby sighed as if content, running his hand over Jacob's bare chest. The fingers felt comforting as they glided over his hard pecs. Did Jacob really want to give this up? Did he want to leave the man beside him to grieve his loss for years to come? Would Shelby grieve his loss that long?

"I'm curious," Jacob started as he stared at the dresser on the other side of the room. "What's involved in a conversion?"

He felt Shelby begin to tremble next to him. It was just a slight shake of his body, but enough for Jacob to know Shelby had been caught off guard.

"You're put into a sort of sleep, and then the prince bites you. He gives you his blood as well and you drink it."

That was it? No dying to be reborn? Hell, Jacob had all kinds of scenarios playing through his mind of being killed in many different ways and then being drained until only a teaspoon of his blood was left. What Shelby described didn't sound so bad.

"And then when you wake up, you're so hungry your gut hurts."

Now that didn't sound too pleasant. "How long does the pain last?"

"Until you feed."

"From you?"

Shelby nodded, his hair brushing along Jacob's shoulder. Jacob shifted a little, wondering if he could really do this. Holding out for science to cure him wasn't working out so well. His time was running short. Either he agreed to be converted or Jacob's days were numbered, and those numbers didn't go very high.

"And I'll be cured?"

Shelby nodded again and then sat up, his licorice-black eyes filled with hope and uncertainty. He could see Shelby was dying to ask if Jacob would do it, be converted. Jacob pulled Shelby down to him, kissing his soft lips. "I'll do it."

Shelby smiled into his kiss, excited energy bubbling and snapping all around him like a happy lightning storm. "Are you sure?"

Jacob nodded. "Right after you ride my cock."

Shelby laughed with joy as he pulled back and quickly divested his pajama bottoms. Jacob grinned when he saw Shelby's erection jutting out. It seemed that Jacob choosing to become a vampire turned the man on. The head of his dick was a deep purple, and the slit was shiny with pre-cum.

Curling his fingers around the erection, Jacob gave a slight stroke, encouraging Shelby to move closer with his callused hand. The shaft felt like steel wrapped in silk as his thumb caressed the skin. Jacob continued to tug until Shelby was standing in front of him, his palms flat against the wall.

The vampire frowned down at him, a look of confusion on his face. Jacob gave a soft chuckle and then leaned forward, taking Shelby's cock into his mouth. Shelby's legs quivered as Jacob ran his hands around the man's hips and cupped his ass, pushing the man's body closer.

He didn't need energy to sit on the bed and suck cock. Nope, no energy at all. Air swooshed from his nose as he sucked the thick length down his throat and then worked his throat muscles.

Shelby whimpered, his movements jumpy as Jacob pressed his finger into Shelby's body. He used his left hand to massage Shelby's balls, making sure every part of Shelby's body below the waist was being touched, rubbed, or sucked. He wanted every part of Shelby stimulated to his touch.

Shelby leaned into Jacob, lips half parted as his hair fell over his eyes, soft, luxurious looking in the low lighting as he gazed down at Jacob. His eyes that were already a perfect blackness grew impossibly darker as his fangs appeared below his top lip. The sharp points gleamed, and Jacob wanted to beg to be bitten.

He hollowed his cheeks, giving Shelby a tight seal as the vampire pressed into Jacob's mouth, the heat of Shelby's skin growing hotter.

Jacob inserted another finger, feeling his heart thudding against his ribs as he sucked a vampire's cock. The thought hit him out of nowhere, but Jacob wasn't repulsed. After all, it was Shelby.

Shelby rolled his hips, moaning above him. The sound washed over Jacob, making him suck harder. He was surprised when the cock left his mouth, Shelby pulling back enough for Jacob's exploring fingers to leave his ass.

Straddling Jacob's hips, Shelby leaned in to take a kiss, his sweet breath caressing Jacob like a warm wind. He smiled while their lips touched, the shyest, sweetest smile, and Jacob lost control. His fingers gripped Shelby's hips, lifting the small man. He didn't have to move. Shelby reached behind his body and guided Jacob's cock to his ass.

"My mate," Shelby whispered as he leaned his face close to Jacob, his lips brushing Jacob's cheek. His tongue flicked over his lips, moistening them before a featherlight kiss was brushed over Jacob's lips.

His cock jerked at the action, his balls pulling close to his body as Shelby began to move forward and then back, his hole milking Jacob's cock like a tight-fitting glove. Jacob brought his legs up, planting his feet as Shelby swiveled his hips like a sultry dance, making his own cock graze against Jacob's flesh.

Shelby's lips were half parted as they ghosted down Jacob's neck, his hair brushing Jacob's skin. The black, silky strands made Jacob's neck tingle as Shelby traced Jacob's jugular with his tongue.

It picked up in beat, as if his body were begging to be bitten. Jacob panted, wondering how someone so much shorter and slimmer than him had such complete control over his mind, body, and heart.

Jacob knew Shelby owned him. There was no question about that.

"I promise to show you the benefits of being a vampire, even in bed." He grinned slightly as he pulled back, his hips still grinding over Jacob's body, his cock lodging deeper.

"Bite me," he begged low when Shelby moved his tongue away.

Shelby shook his head. "When you become a vampire, I will gladly drink from you, mate, but not before then. You are too weak, Jacob," Shelby said softly, his black eyes sparkling. "Not before then," he repeated.

Jacob smashed his lips into Shelby's, thrusting his cock into Shelby's ass as fire raced through his blood, making Jacob cry out as his orgasm was ripped from his body.

And then his head began to swoon. Small prickles of white light danced before his eyes as his heart rate sped up and then slowed down, the beats too slow, too dangerously slow. He glanced at Shelby, his eyes growing wide. "I think you need to convert me now, Shelby."

Shelby sat there for a moment, looking perplexed, and then he was scrambling from Jacob's lap. "Your heart, why isn't it beating like it should?"

Shelby's words and movements were sluggish as Jacob tried to lift his hand, but expending even that small amount of energy had become too much. He fixed his lips to speak, but he became disoriented. "I'm scared," he managed to garble out.

"I'm going to get Christian. Don't you fucking die on me, Jacob Marshall!" Shelby leaned over the bed, caressing his hand down the side of Jacob's cheek. "Don't be scared, mate. I'll get the prince."

Jacob tried to nod, but his head slumped sideways instead. Was this supposed to happen? What the hell was wrong with him? He concentrated on his arm, but no amount of willing the thing to move made it happen. Would he die before the prince converted him?

Glancing toward the door, Jacob wasn't sure he would. He tried to call out for Shelby, but the word was nothing more than a gurgle. His heart was failing. Jacob could hear the beat come slower and slower as he sat there with his back pressed into the headboard, his head slouched to the side.

Thump. His heart was struggling to work, struggling to beat. Jacob could feel it. But he knew it wouldn't last. He knew this had been coming, but he hadn't expected it to come so quickly. He thought he had more time.

Thump. Jacob glanced at the open door and prayed Shelby got Christian here in time. His eyes slid closed as a soft breath left his lips.

Stutter.

* * * *

Shelby appeared in his bedroom beside Christian. He gasped when he saw Jacob slumped over, unmoving. "No!" he shouted as he jumped up onto the bed, bloodred tears flowing from his eyes as he pulled Jacob into his arms, cradling him, rocking him.

"Give him to me," Christian said as he pulled Jacob from Shelby's arms.

"No, Prince, no!" Shelby shouted as he tried to hold on to his mate. Jacob wasn't moving, his lips slightly blue. Shelby fought the prince to get to his mate. Jacob was dead, and Shelby was losing his sanity as Christian pulled Jacob away from the bed. "Give him to me, please," Shelby sobbed.

"His heart is still beating, weakly, but there is a pulse, young one. Let me save him."

Shelby slid from the bed, dropping to his knees next to his mate as his hands trembled at his lips. "Can you convert him?"

Christian laid Jacob out on the rug, Mango lying down next to Jacob, whimpering. Christian grabbed the sheet from the bed, covering Jacob's exposed groin as he leaned forward and bit into Jacob's neck.

Shelby realized that he had run into the hallway naked, and still was. He would be worried about his humiliation later. Right now he was scared out of his mind that he would lose his mate. What had taken so long was convincing Christian that Jacob had agreed to become a vampire. The prince didn't look convinced until he touched Shelby's head and saw for himself the conversation Shelby and Jacob had had. Once the prince saw that Jacob had agreed, he rushed to Shelby's bedroom.

He sat there watching, his hand rubbing over Mango's head gently. Jacob was so still, like a corpse. A shudder raced through Shelby's body at the thought. His mate's complexion wasn't the soft combination of peach and tan that Shelby loved. It was pale and tinged with a slight coloring of grey.

This worried him more than anything.

Christian leaned back, slicing his wrist open with his fangs, and then let the blood drip down into Jacob's mouth.

Nothing happened.

Shelby held his breath, his eyes fixated on the blood pooling around Jacob's lips and then overflowing to slide down the side of his face. *Jacob should be drinking. He should be swallowing.* But Jacob lay there with his eyes closed, the blood sitting in his mouth like an overfilled cup.

Mango jerked when Jacob inhaled sharply, the blood disappearing down his throat, and then he fell silent again.

"Does that mean he is going to be all right?" Shelby asked as he leaned closer, seeing that the blood that had pooled in Jacob's mouth was gone. Only the crimson color around the edges remained.

"The blood has entered his body. Give it time, Shelby. It should start working very soon."

That didn't answer his question. The word *should* made him worry more, not less. Jacob didn't have a pulse. He wasn't moving. It was a wait-and-see game now as Shelby stayed beside his mate.

"You know when he wakes he'll need to feed, young one."

Shelby nodded as his fingers caressed through Jacob's short hair. The man looked like he was in a peaceful sleep now. As if he had just lay down on the carpet and closed his eyes. Well, except for the red tinting his lips. "Thank you."

He felt the displaced air as Christian vanished from his bedroom. Shelby crawled around Jacob's body and stretched out beside it,

Mango lying on the other side of Jacob as Shelby curled close, close enough to feel Jacob's skin touching his as he closed his eyes. Maybe getting some sleep would make the wait a little less tense.

Shelby must have fallen asleep. The metal shutters were lifted, the moonlight spilling into his bedroom, washing over his and Jacob's naked bodies. He sat up, placing his hand on Jacob's chest. His heart jumped when Jacob's did.

Laying his head on Jacob's hard chest, he heard his mate's heart thump once again. Normally a human didn't have to die to become a vampire, but it seemed Jacob had. Shelby had never heard of anything like this happening before. It was pretty much a given that if a person died, they were dead.

There was no grey area.

But Jacob had defied that reasoning as his heart began to slowly beat stronger, his chest convulsing with the beat. Shelby moved his head away when Jacob took in a strong lungful of air. Mango whimpered and moved away. His canine eyes held fear.

Shelby yelped when he was thrown to his back, Jacob's light-brown eyes gleaming down at him, filled with hunger and lust. He bared his neck as Jacob leaned his head back, his brand-new fangs gleaming before he struck.

Mango barked, pacing around their bodies, as if confused on what to do. Shelby reached out with his mind and glamored the dog into silence. He hoped it worked. He had never glamored an animal before.

Mango lay down, his head resting on his front paws as he whimpered. Was the dog afraid for Shelby or worried for Jacob?

Jacob pulled in large swallows of blood, his fingers curled around the back of Shelby's head. Thank goodness he was a vampire, or Jacob would have drained him. After a few moments, though, he pinched Jacob's nose and pushed him away. "Enough."

Jacob licked his lips, his tongue chasing the blood until his lips were clean. Shelby watched as his mate's eyes slowly began to focus.

They morphed from wild to intelligent. A smile formed on Jacob's lips as his fangs appeared proudly. "I see it worked."

Shelby launched himself into Jacob's arms, sobbing with relief. His mate hadn't died. He was whole and squatting right here in front of him, his heartbeat strong. Shelby was surprised Jacob hadn't fallen back with the forward momentum of his body. It only showed Shelby that Jacob was much stronger now, more agile.

"You came back to me," he whimpered into Jacob's shoulder. Shelby inhaled. The smell of sickness was gone. There was nothing left of the illness. The only thing Shelby smelled was Jacob's sweet scent. The smooth, solid grip of Jacob's hand wrapped around Shelby's shoulder. It was a comforting weight on Shelby's shoulder as he nuzzled closer to his mate. He could feel the strength pulling at him, drawing him in.

Shelby let it.

Fear had gripped him with such a cold, hard grip that letting it melt away was such a glorious feeling.

"I'm here, my little vampire." Jacob ran his hands over Shelby's head. "I'm not going anywhere."

Shelby shivered at the promise. He was going to make sure Jacob made good on it, too. He never wanted to feel the heavy loss again. He pushed and then pushed a little harder until Jacob became unstable and crashed to his ass, Shelby following him down. "How do you feel?" he asked as he began to pepper wet kisses over Jacob's face.

"Great," Jacob said as he laughed. "Fantastic."

Shelby wasted no time. He plunged his ass onto Jacob's cock, biting into his mate's neck at the same time. With everything going on lately, he hadn't fed. Shelby was starving. His eyes grew wide as one minute he was sitting atop Jacob, and the next he was pinned to the floor. It had been one fluid motion, quick, and hell if Shelby could even remember seeing Jacob move at all.

The grunts filled the room as Jacob took him harder, more brutal, and Shelby was enjoying every second of it as his tongue snaked out and lapped at the skin, closing the twin pinpricks.

Jacob almost bent him in half, his knees close to his ears as Jacob's hips snapped in quick bursts. Without touching his cock, Shelby shouted, his cock erupting. His hole ached and burned and felt as if it were stretched to its limits, but apparently Jacob was testing his stamina, because he kept right on fucking Shelby, his fingers gripping Shelby's calves tightly.

Shelby wrapped his ankles around Jacob's head, pulling hard, bringing his mate's face close enough for Jacob to see the smile on his lips. Jacob's light-brown eyes turned to a brilliant coppery color as he bared his fangs, his hips slowly moving back, and then he slammed forward, meeting Shelby's challenge and then some.

Damn, he was going to regret this later, or more precisely, his ass was going to regret this. There was not only pleasure radiating throughout his lower half, but a dull pain as well. Jacob wasn't joking around. The newborn vampire meant business as his cock split Shelby open with each tantalizing thrust.

Shelby laughed with triumph as he swung his legs that had been around Jacob's neck sideways, his vampire falling with the swing of momentum. Shelby managed to untangle his legs and wrap them around Jacob's waist, using the strength in his legs to pull Jacob closer, drive his cock deeper.

"Acrobatics?" Jacob asked as he slid his arms around Shelby's frame. "Because I know you are not fighting me for power here."

Shelby smiled. "What if I am?"

Jacob's smile was wide, sensual, and downright dirty as he wickedly smiled at Shelby. He rolled, pinning Shelby beneath him once more before he bit into Shelby's neck, squelching any plans he may have had to gain the upper hand.

Shelby groaned loud as he felt Jacob's cock pulsing in his ass at the same time the skin was being sucked at his neck. The dual combination sent Shelby gliding over the edge once more.

His brow rose when he felt the deep rumble of Jacob chuckling as he licked Shelby's wound closed.

"What's so funny?" he asked as Jacob pulled back to stare down at him. His light-brown eyes were back, set evenly in the center of his newly pale face. The man was breathtakingly beautiful as a vampire.

As Shelby knew he would be.

"Everything," Jacob announced and pulled his soft cock free. He stood and held his hand out, pulling Shelby to his feet in one quick motion, almost lifting him off of his feet. Shelby had a feeling Jacob was enjoying his newfound powers a little too much. If the man had raised his arm any higher, Shelby would have been dangling in the air.

Jacob released Shelby and shot across the room so quickly with preternatural speed that even Shelby, who had excellent vision, almost missed the movement. One moment he was standing next to Shelby, the next he was across the room.

Show-off.

Mango's head was just now turning, just now spotting his master on the other side, standing by the bathroom door. The dog looked confused. Shelby laughed.

"Will it always be like this, or do I feel this way because I'm newly converted?" Jacob asked right before he appeared at Shelby's side.

"The elated feelings are from your conversion. But your quickness, agility, and"—Shelby could feel his face heating as he glanced up at Jacob—"your stamina will only get better. You'll learn how to hone them."

"My stamina, huh?" Jacob asked before going into the bathroom, his tightly muscled ass making Shelby's fangs itch. He had created a monster. Shelby could see that now. Being a newborn, Jacob just might fuck him into an early grave.

And he couldn't wait.

Chapter Nine

Christian flipped through the file in his hand, glancing over the report the lead annihilator had prepared. Not only had the vampire given him the statistics on the alarming rate of rogue vampires, but he also had given him quite a large bill for his services.

Christian closed the file and handed it to Christo. Let his second take care of the paperwork.

"If those numbers are satisfactory, we can finish the job."

The prince assumed the man was talking about the financial side to this, because the number of rogues populating his city was anything but satisfying. He wanted to tell the man that the amount was highway robbery, but he also knew that the best had been sent to him.

The lead annihilator was from down south, Gallagher's Coven. They were deeper into voodoo rituals and practices, but he didn't think the man would shake chicken bones at anyone. The two standing off to the right were from the north, somewhere in the Dakotas. Their appearances were distinctly Native American. Christian didn't think he had ever seen a vampire with caramel-colored skin before.

And the last two were from Los Angeles. The damn fools even wore bandanas on their heads. But he was assured by the coven leaders who sent the men that they were the very best. He would soon find out.

"Your offer is acceptable. But you will only be paid when I see the population of infected vampires lower to almost nonexistent." Christian wasn't foolish enough to believe that they would all disappear. Even a cockroach survived nuclear attacks. Some would get away, but he was hoping to solve this problem without awakening his brothers.

Gavino, the lead annihilator, nodded, a cocky half smile on his lips. "No problem."

Christian hoped the man was half as good as his self-confident smile indicated. He waved them from his office, taking a seat at the table.

"Do you think they can do it?" Nija asked. Christian's shoulders lifted slightly as he stared at the door they had just exited.

"Only time will tell." He turned, looking back at the men sitting around the table. "Now where were we?"

* * * *

Jacob held on to the leash as he walked down the street of the residential neighborhood, enjoying the fresh night air. The moon was only a sliver in the sky, clouds barely wisps as the sound of singing crickets sounded all around them. It was peaceful. He grabbed Shelby's hand, giving it a light squeeze as they walked Mango.

The houses in this area were about a half a mile apart from each other, affording the owners privacy in this heavily wooded neighborhood.

Observing Shelby as he walked beside him, Jacob noticed a smile of contentment on the man's face that had been there all evening. He knew it was just because of the well-placed cock he'd given his mate earlier. The man seemed to just float along next to him, happy with the world.

Jacob wrapped an arm around his little vampire, knowing the man was happy Jacob hadn't bitten the dust. That made two of them. He may have thought that everyone had their time to die, but come on, longevity behind his wildest dreams? Not even he was foolish enough to pass that by.

It must have been the sickness clouding his mind at the time.

Mango pulled at the leash, and then came trotting back over to Jacob, walking beside him obediently when a man pulled into one of the driveways and got out to check his mailbox. There was nothing threatening about checking a mailbox, so why did the hairs on his neck stand up and a cold wind blow down his spine?

Slowing his steps, Jacob deliberately began to pull Shelby behind him. The little vampire looked up at him confusingly, but didn't fight to stay next to Jacob. Mango even began to give off a low growl.

Jacob pushed Shelby away from him as a gun appeared in the man's hands. Mango was going ballistic, barking and pulling at his leash to get at the stranger as the sound of bullets exploded in the peaceful night.

Releasing the leash, Jacob used his newfound speed to run toward the man and disarm him in a span of a second. The man looked shocked and paled slightly as he looked from Jacob to the gun that he no longer possessed.

"Who are you?" Jacob snarled as he pressed the gun under the man's chin, the metal pushing the man's head back.

"You're one of them," he said as if surprised. If the man hadn't known, that meant he was gunning for Shelby. That didn't make Jacob feel any better. He wanted to pull the trigger so badly that his fingers itched. Why shouldn't he? The guy had shot at them. It would only serve him right and eliminate the threat to Shelby. But Jacob wasn't a coldblooded killer. Not today anyway.

"I asked you a question."

The guy swallowed, the gun moving slightly under the man's whiskered chin. "I can't tell you."

"He has to be a hunter," Shelby said as he pushed to his feet, brushing his hair from his eyes. Mango walked right to Shelby's side. Jacob was glad the dog recognized Shelby as one of his masters. The German Shepherd stood vigilantly next to the small vampire as Shelby gazed at them with large, frightened black eyes.

It didn't take a genius to figure out what Shelby was saying. "So you thought you would pop Shelby and then what, get into your car and drive away?"

Shooting the man was looking better and better. Jacob had to fight not to tear the man's throat out. Images of the prince killing the intruder that day in the front foyer played in Jacob's mind as he used his weight to press the man into his car.

"They are an infectious disease, and it's only getting worse." The man's face switched from shock to hatred. "There are vampires everywhere now, killing innocent human beings, draining them dry. They have to be stopped. You have to be stopped."

The man was talking about the rogues, but Jacob knew not all vampires were blind killing machines. He had met quite a few decent ones, not only at the club, but at the manor as well. He agreed that the scourge of the vampire world needed to be stopped, but this wasn't the way. Randomly shooting suspected vampires was nothing but coldblooded murder.

Shelby could have been killed. And that thought twisted Jacob's gut into a tightly woven knot. Jacob bared his fangs, making sure the stranger felt the implication. "If you sneak up on anyone else, I'll use your own gun to blow your fucking head off. Get the hell out of here."

Taking a step back, Jacob gave the man room enough to get into his car and drive away. It may have been an unintelligent thing to do. The man may come back to kill him, but Jacob had also seen the fear in the guy's eyes. Call him a sucker.

"Let's get home," Jacob said as he stuffed the gun into his waistband, making sure the safety was engaged first. He didn't want to blow an ass cheek off if he tripped. Shelby quickly joined him as they headed back toward the manor.

Jacob couldn't deny that he had been scared shitless, but adrenaline was pumping through his system at the idea that he had been able to defend his little vampire. He hadn't been winded or tired.

In fact, he had felt strength inside of him that hadn't been there before, fueling his muscles for the fight.

"Thank you," Shelby said as he grabbed Mango's leash, "for saving my life."

Jacob leaned toward Shelby and kissed his temple. "I didn't get converted to walk this life alone."

Shelby grinned up at him, but there was tension in every crease of the man's face. Even his deep dimples wavered slightly. They reached the manor quicker than humanly possible, vampire speed. Jacob escorted Shelby and Mango inside and then went looking for Logan. He found the shifter around back, scanning the wooded area.

"A hunter shot at Shelby and I on our walk."

Logan rested his arms loosely across his chest as he regarded Jacob. "Did you kill him?"

Jacob pulled the gun from his waistband and handed it to the shifter. "No."

"Newborns." Logan tsked. "Being a newly born vampire, you should have blindly torn his throat out, Jacob. Interesting."

Interesting? What did that mean? Jacob waved a hand at the gun as he turned to walk away. "A gift." He ran his hand through his hair, his hand shaky as he finally let go of the long held breath. Damn it, Shelby could have been killed tonight, and he let the bastard go. Jacob wasn't sure why he had done that. Every cell inside of him had pushed Jacob to kill the man, but he had resisted.

Why?

He had no clue why he hadn't ripped the bastard's throat out. But something had stopped him. Morals? Scruples? Standards? Since when in the hell did he possess any of those? He had done some things in his human life he hadn't been proud of. So why hadn't he blown the man's head off when he was clearly a threat to Shelby?

Pushing the door open, Jacob saw Shelby and Mango waiting for him in the front room.

"Do you want to go to the club?" Shelby asked.

Jacob should. Maybe dancing or fighting someone would dispel all of this agitated energy flowing through him.

It was worth a shot anyway.

After feeding and giving Mango his water, Jacob left for the club with Shelby. The all-too-familiar scents hit him as soon as they walked into the club, leather, body sweat, and alcohol. He hadn't been a fan of it when he was a human, and Jacob still wasn't a fan of the odors now. The club was jam-packed with half-naked dancers.

Jacob grabbed Shelby, twirling him onto his dance floor as the energy inside of him flowed and ebbed, making Jacob feel as though he could conquer the world. Shelby twirled, danced, and laughed as Jacob spun his little vampire around. His new lease on life was fabulous. He wasn't even winded after the third song. Shelby's face lit up as if a candle had been lit behind his skin. It was glowing.

"I love you," Jacob said as he cupped the small man's face and kissed him. "I love everything about you, Shelby." He loved Shelby so much his chest ached.

"I love you, too," Shelby whispered against his lips.

Eli brought Jacob a glass of water, and with complete joy, Jacob shook his head. "I don't need it, but thanks anyway."

Eli cocked his brow, and Jacob showed off his fangs proudly. Eli chuckled and headed away. Life was good.

After about five songs, Jacob excused himself and went outside for some fresh air. He may have the stamina to dance the night away, but he still became sweaty in the thick crowd. He nodded at the bouncer, Harley, as he walked outside. Jacob tilted his head back and smiled up at the stars. They were simply stunning.

"I see you're back for more."

Jacob lowered his head to see Taras standing over by a car. Déjà vu hit him as he smiled to himself. This time the little shit was going to learn a lesson in bullying people. "I have no idea what you mean."

Taras had a smug smile on his face as he turned toward Jacob, his stance casual as if he planned on putting Jacob on his ass once more.

Not going to happen.

"I told you Shelby was going to pay for what he did to me."

"And what about what you did to him?" Jacob inquired as he walked closer. "Or have you forgotten that you tried to force him?"

"No, I didn't. He is just a big-ass cry baby. I only wanted to have a little fun." Taras shrugged. "It's not my fault the man can't handle a little bondage."

Jacob hid his fangs, although they were aching to tear this little punk's throat out. Taras was smiling at him, but his eyes held something more serious in them. As if he were planning on really hurting Jacob this time.

He would never understand men like Taras. They took and took, never thinking of anyone but themselves. And when someone stood up to them, they felt as if the other person was in the wrong.

The man would never learn.

And that was truly sad.

"No means no, Taras."

"You sound like those damn antirape commercials. It means yes if I want it, whatever *it* may be at the time."

"Are you really that self-inflated, insensitive, and self-serving?"

Taras chuckled and gave a one-sided shrug. "That's me."

It pissed Jacob off that Taras was so proud of those facts. He truly was a monster in a compact body. *They must come in all sizes.*

Pint size for Taras.

"I'm warning you to leave him alone." Just because Jacob was a vampire now, he wasn't looking to prove himself. He was still the same man, only stronger, faster…okay, so he had changed in some ways, but not in his personality.

"And if I choose not to?" Taras challenged, his eyes sparkling at the thought of a fight. Jacob could just tell the man was salivating for one. People like Taras always were.

"I'll tear your nads off and shove them down your goddamn throat."

Taras laughed, and it slid over Jacob like an itchy blanket. The man was really asking for it. And wouldn't the little shit be surprised when he found out Jacob was a vampire. The man should have been able to smell the change in Jacob. Shelby told him that vampires could distinguish between beings. The man must not have had his sniffer activated. He was too busy priding himself on bullying what he thought was a human.

Jacob actually pitied the man. It had to be a cold, lonely life to push everyone away the way Taras was doing. Instead of making friends, he found comfort in enemies. If he hadn't done what he had done to Shelby, Jacob just might have tried to chip away at the ice around the man's heart.

Too bad Taras had tried, and was still trying, to hurt Shelby. That was a deal breaker in his book. "Go make a friend somewhere, Taras. I'm not in the mood. My night has been going great so far." He knew he had struck a chord when Taras's eyes became inflamed. The man snarled as he flew at Jacob with that preternatural speed only a vampire possessed.

Jacob easily dodged the man, stepping aside at the last second. He really didn't want to fight the man. He just wanted Taras to leave him and Shelby alone.

"How?" Taras looked stunned as he spun around.

Jacob grinned, showing off his new dental work. Taras's eyes grew round, and then they narrowed as he came after Jacob again. It was as if it were a personal insult to the man for Jacob to be a vampire.

When Taras's arm slung out, claws exposed, Jacob grabbed Taras's arm and swung it behind the man's back, twisting it painfully. "Stop this."

"What's going on?" Harley asked as he walked over to them. The man was a few inches taller than Jacob, brawny, with black hair brushing his shoulders. Why did all vampires seem to have black hair and eyes? Only Harley's hair was pulled back with a leather thong to rest on his back.

"We were just discussing Taras never coming back here again. Weren't we?" Jacob asked as he yanked the man's arm up another inch, just enough to inflict pain, but not enough to break the damn thing.

"Taras, I don't think Christian is going to be happy you're coming around here starting shit," Harley said as he tapped the small device wrapped around his ear.

Jacob released Taras, pushing the man away from him. Before he could tell the punk to get out of here, Christian was outside the club and the man didn't look too damn happy.

"I see you haven't learned anything from your last punishment," Christian said as he pulled Taras toward him by the blue collar of the man's shirt. "What have you been up to this time?"

"Nothing," Taras said innocently.

Christian looked as if he didn't believe the man. So the prince was intelligent. *Good to know.*

The prince placed his hand on Taras's head, and the man wiggled, trying to get free. Jacob just stood there watching, wondering what Christian was doing. It became obvious when the prince snarled and yanked Taras's shirt back and forth. "You threatened Shelby and physically harmed Jacob when he was weak?"

Jacob didn't care to be reminded how weak he had been. It was a blow to his damn ego. *Ouch.* A man did have his pride after all.

"I—"

"Silence," Christian hissed. The prince turned his head toward Jacob. That demonic look was back. "Name his punishment."

"No," Jacob said as he shook his head. There was no way the prince of vampires was laying that kind of shit at Jacob's feet.

"Name. His. Punishment."

It was an order. Jacob could feel some sort of push against his mind. The prince was making him do this. *Bastard.*

"I may be just that, but you will name his punishment for harming you and threatening your mate. It is our way."

What the hell. The man could use a good dose of humble pie. "I know exactly what his punishment should be."

Oh, this was going to be good.

Chapter Ten

Shelby froze when he walked toward the door in search of Jacob and saw Taras standing next to Harley. What the hell was he doing here? Shelby wasn't sure what was going on, but panic started to rise inside of him like a tsunami ready to tear him down.

He cocked his head, moving a little closer when he saw the halfhearted smile on the vampire's face as a human couple walked through the doorway into the club.

"Enjoy your time at The Manacle," Taras said as he waved the humans in. "There's dancing, drinks, and food."

Okay, Shelby had to be stuck in some sort of strange, Dr. Evil, warped universe. There was no way Taras was a damn door greeter. Fate wasn't that kind to Shelby. Not when it pertained to the bane of his existence.

"Hello, Shelby. I hope you are doing fine this evening."

Shelby stepped back, afraid Taras would morph into some sort of deranged clown and attack him. This shit was scary. He could see the flecks of anger in Taras's eyes, but the faked smile held firm.

"What in the hell are you doing?" he asked softly as he glanced from Taras to Harley.

"Having pleasantries," he answered.

Okay, Shelby was officially scared out of his mind. This was *not* Taras. It had to be a clone, a twin, something other than the pompous jackass who had insulted him and felt he was superior to all others.

"He's being punished," Harley said as he chuckled. "He should know by now not to piss the prince off."

Ah, that explained everything. Shelby had thought that maybe the universe had shifted and good and evil had changed sides. He inched past Taras, careful not to touch the strange man as he walked outside.

Pretending to be nice and actually being nice were totally different. He still didn't trust the man. He spotted Jacob deep in conversation with Christian in the parking lot. Did Taras's punishment have something to do with Jacob?

He approached the two men, standing next to Jacob quietly. Their voices became hushed when Shelby came into view. Damn, that could give a guy a complex real quick. "Is everything all right?"

Christian smiled at him as Jacob drew an arm around Shelby, pulling him in close. "Everything is fine, my little vampire," Jacob replied.

Christian chuckled at the endearment. Hopefully that was what he was laughing at. Shelby froze in horrifying fear when he glanced toward the edge of the parking lot and saw a horde of rogues heading their way.

Those things never hunted in packs, groups, whatever the hell the word was. "Prince!" Shelby shouted as he pointed, but Christian was already moving, waving his arm for the humans who were outside of the club to get their asses inside quickly.

The humans looked confused, but ran inside. Shelby watched as every able-bodied vampire pushed past the running humans and came outside. Shelby shuddered when he saw Harley close the steel door to the club, locking all the humans inside.

"Get under the car," Jacob shouted as he tried to push Shelby toward the ground.

"I–I can fight," Shelby shouted in the chaos, watching as the rogues drew near. The smell of death and fresh blood entered the parking lot ahead of the rogues, as if they had fed well before coming here. He saw some rogues climbing over cars, others walking around them, all heading in their direction.

"Someone is controlling them," Christian said and then roared as his fangs elongated until the tips were resting against his chin and black claws erupted from his fingernails. His skin began to take on a purplish hue, his height growing until he was two feet taller.

Even though Christian was as nice as a father to Shelby, damn if the man wasn't a frightening sight.

"I'm so glad he is on our side," Jacob said as the first wave of rogues attacked.

Shelby was instantly pinned to the ground, a rogue sitting on his chest. Unquenchable hunger slid through the creature's eyes as his foul breath made Shelby breathe through his nose. But even breathing through his nose, Shelby still tasted the acrid smell. It was like a side of already-spoiled beef had been sitting out on a hot, sweltering summer day in a metal Dumpster.

It was that bad.

"Young blood," the rogue said with glee as he poised his head to strike. Shelby knew he was outweighed and going to die. He was not graceful as he smashed the palm of his hand into the rogue's jaw, pushing his sharp fangs away.

"And feisty. You're going to taste so damn good."

"Not today," Jacob said as he yanked the rogue from off of Shelby's chest. Shelby got a quick glance around at the fighting before Jacob grabbed Shelby and nearly shoved him into a car. Instead, he was pushed under the vehicle.

"Do not come out for anything!" Jacob shouted before his head disappeared, and all Shelby saw was the man's shoes. They were black, leather, and looked damned comfortable. And why on earth was he admiring his mate's comfortable-looking shoes?

It was a blow to Shelby's ego, but he knew he wasn't as strong as the rogues or older vampires. He could bench-press the car he was lying under, but he couldn't beat a damn rogue, not this many at least. One on one, he may have a chance.

Shelby covered his ears when he heard Christian roar. The sound was deafening, even under the car. He could hear hissing, snapping, shouts, slamming, and things breaking. And he could see everyone's feet as well. He saw Sutton's full body when the bouncer hit the ground, fighting a rogue off.

Shelby glanced around, trying to find something to help get the creature off of Sutton. The only thing around him was car parts.

Someone was going to be pissed as hell.

Shelby reached up and pulled one of the pipes closest to him until it gave. The end was jagged, the metal slightly rusty. Pulling his arm all the way back, he rammed the piece of metal forward and shoved it straight into the rogue's side. It gave Sutton the break he needed.

"Thanks," Sutton said as he rolled and got to his feet.

At least he was somewhat useful under this damn heap of metal. Shelby moved away when a rogue dropped to his hands and knees, reaching under the car for him. There was a liquid dangerous look in the thing's eyes as he tried to crawl under the car. Shelby referred to them as things, creatures, savages because in his eyes, they were no longer a part of his race. They were something that should be burned until their flesh smoked in the fresh morning sun.

He reached up, yanking another pipe down from the underbelly of the car, swinging the best he could in the confined space. He knew he wasn't going to hurt the creature where he was lying, so he rolled, keeping the pipe firmly in his hand as he jumped to his feet.

The urge to disseminate back to the manor was strong, but that would mean leaving Jacob behind, and Shelby just couldn't do that.

The rogue came around the car, his fangs bared as he leapt toward Shelby. He swung the pipe, almost wrapping it around the thing's head, but it kept right on coming. Fuck, this wasn't good.

As squeamish as Shelby was about the method to kill rogues, he fought to keep his eyes open as his claws extended and his hand burst into the rogue's chest. He curled his fingers around the bastard's heart and yanked his hand back with all his might.

Fucking gross.

Shelby quickly dropped the heart, feeling the need to vomit wash over him. He gagged and then dropped back down to the ground at the same time the dead rogue fell. Shelby scooted back under the car, and then saw the lifeless eyes just staring at him.

Great.

He reached out, pushing the dead rogue's head until it was facing away from him. He just couldn't lie there while the thing stared blankly at him. That was more than he could handle. Shelby turned away, looking straight ahead at the fighting, and wondered how long the battle was going to last.

Why in the hell did all those rogues storm the club? He thought about Christian, about what the man had said. Someone was controlling them, but who? That person would have to be mighty powerful, even more powerful than Christian.

That was indeed a scary thought.

He stilled when he heard the fighting dying down. Who had won? Who was standing in the parking lot now? Biting his bottom lip, Shelby scooted slowly from under the car, glancing around quickly to make sure he wasn't about to be attacked.

Relief flooded through him, washing away his apprehension as he saw Jacob standing by the car Shelby had been hidden under. His mate was a bloody mess, the front of his shirt soaked in blood, but he was alive.

Shelby ran to him, throwing his arms around his vampire as he looked around at the carnage. There were bodies lying everywhere, and not all of them were rogues. Some vampires had lost their lives tonight.

Christian was back to his other form, his vampire form, and looking around as if every life lost tonight impacted him personally. The grief on the man's face was so strong that it felt as though Shelby could reach out and wrap his arms around it.

"Is it over?" Shelby asked the prince. When Christian nodded, Shelby disseminated to the manor, leaving the bloody mess behind.

He walked Jacob to the bathroom, undressing his mate and then pulling him into the shower. Jacob looked a little shell-shocked, as if the bloody battle had been too much for him. He moved along like a zombie, letting Shelby guide him.

Turning the shower on, Shelby grabbed a towel and began to bathe the blood from his mate's skin. He saw that he wasn't blood-free. It clung to his arm from tearing that rogue's heart out, but he was more concerned with cleaning Jacob.

As the water washed the crimson color down the drain, Shelby made sure every inch of Jacob was clean. He wasn't sure his mate could handle it if he saw any blood left on his body.

Next Shelby washed his arm thoroughly, and then his body. Jacob didn't say a word the whole time they were in the shower. He just stared blankly at the shower tiles.

Cutting the water off, Shelby led his mate from the shower and stood there in the middle of the bathroom and dried Jacob off. Guiding him to the bed, Shelby pulled the cream-and-brown blanket back as he laid Jacob down.

Shelby crawled next to his mate and pulled Jacob into his arms, holding him.

* * * *

Jacob jogged down the side of the road. Being a vampire now, he really didn't need the exercise. Shelby told him that the body he had now would be his one and only birthday suit for all eternity. Thank fuck he was well built before he was converted.

It would have sucked to have been an out-of-shape vampire.

But Mango could use the exercise. The German Shepherd was still young, and from the way things were going, would need to stay in shape to haul ass. He may be a natural rogue detector, but that didn't make him invincible.

Running was always a good option when outnumbered.

Jacob also carried the gun he had taken off of the man who had tried to shoot Shelby while checking his damn mail. Although Jacob had a feeling the man didn't even live at that address.

Logan had given it back to him, telling Jacob that he really didn't need it since he was a shifter.

Jacob accepted the gun back. There was nothing wrong with being overprepared.

Shelby had to work tonight, and Jacob really didn't feel like hanging around the club. It was all right once in a while, but every night just wasn't his style. The night was cool, the crickets singing along as Jacob's feet hit the blacktop. Even though he didn't have to jog, it felt good to get out of the manor.

He would never understand how the coven spent most of their time between the manor and The Manacle. There was so much more out here to explore. Hell, he had eternity to travel the globe now.

Too bad he didn't have the cash to make it happen.

Jacob stumbled and caught himself when his foot hit a dip in the road. He glanced back, wondering how he had missed that. He was supposed to be quick, graceful now that he was among the undead.

Was he undead?

He had died.

So he must be undead.

That was a creepy thought.

Mango barked and began to pull back on his leash. The hairs down his spine were standing straight up, and his ears were laid flat.

Never a good sign.

Jacob glanced around but only saw the quiet, wooded, upscale neighborhood all around him. The wind blew slightly, and a few lights were on in the house closest to him, but there was no other sound except the crickets...and Mango's low growl.

"What is it, boy?" Jacob asked as his eyes darted around. It would be a good idea to turn around and run, but he didn't want whoever, or whatever, at his back. That wouldn't be wise.

So he just stood there like a sitting duck and waited for an attack. One of the lights went out in the house off to his left, and the leaves rustled, but still nothing.

Jacob turned, heading back toward the manor. He had hoped that he could get out tonight without incident, but it wasn't turning out that way. No one shot a gun at him, but the silence was even more threatening to him for some reason.

When lights cut a path in front of him, telling him there was a car coming up the road from behind, Jacob moved to the sidewalk and unzipped the gun from the pocket in his light jacket. He tensed, slowed, and kept his eyes straight ahead.

The car passed him by, Jacob seeing the red taillights as it wove around the corner. It was just a car. Only a damn car. He shoved the gun back into his pocket and zipped it back into its hiding place.

Maybe Mango had spotted a deer or some other creature that roamed the woods. He was a city dog after all. It might not have been a preternatural being, or a hunter.

There should be a damn handbook on how to survive once a person is converted. The shit was dangerous.

As they rounded the corner, Jacob saw the car that had passed him by. It was just sitting in the middle of the road, motor running, and taillights bright. Whoever it was, they had their foot on the brake.

Shelby hadn't taught him that neat little trick of disseminating yet, so Jacob was stuck either walking past the idling car or running up into the woods and weaving his way back to the manor through the trees…and anything else that was hiding behind the branches.

Both choices left a bad taste in his mouth.

He knew not too many vampires drove. They liked popping in and out of places too damn much.

Again, he was seriously going to learn that trick.

Removing the small handheld gun once more, Jacob kept a tight grip on the butt as he walked slowly past the car. Mango began to growl once more, his ears laid back.

Jacob quickly glanced into the car, making sure he wasn't an easy target with a gun pointed at his chest when he saw that the car was empty.

If no one was behind the wheel, then how were the brake lights shining so brightly? Glancing around and seeing no one, Jacob walked over to the car. He moved back hurriedly when he saw a brick pressed down on the brake pedal.

What the hell was going on?

"Don't move."

Jacob froze, but the German Shepherd barked loudly and yanked on his leash. He inched his hand forward that held the gun, keeping it out of the person's view. Hopefully they hadn't seen it.

"You should have shot me," the man said with a smile in his voice. Jacob didn't have to see the man to hear the humor in the tone.

So much for doing the right thing. How does that saying go? No good deed goes unpunished? Yeah, that's it.

Jacob now knew he was dealing with a human. He felt a little better about the situation, barely.

"What do you want?" he asked as if he didn't know. He knew. The man wanted to paint the blacktop with Jacob's brain. But clarifying things didn't hurt.

His thumb slid the safety off. Thank goodness he knew how to shoot a gun. He never claimed to be a candidate for sainthood. He held the gun tightly in his hand, ready for bear as he tried to pinpoint the hunter's position.

"I want your kind eradicated. What do you think the human population would do if they found out that there were vampires living among them? Do you think they would welcome you with open arms and give you voting rights?"

Jacob knew the human population wouldn't. When faced with the unknown, most human beings panicked and killed. Some captured and studied, but that was even less palatable. "And you're going to be the one to tell the world we exist?" he asked.

"It's a possibility," the man said. "How much do you want to bet our small hunting group would get full support from any and every radical group across the country?"

Jacob had no doubt that the bloodshed would not only be countrywide, but worldwide. Anyone with messed-up teeth would probably be staked. Vigilante groups would crop up like a damn disease, killing all in the name of mankind.

Woo-hoo.

But he was listening to the freak and had heard that the vampire hunting group was small. If he didn't decorate the pavement with his brain matter, he would have to let Christian know this. Jacob inhaled deeply, feeling his new senses tingling as he tried to pinpoint exactly where the hunter was standing. If he could figure that part out, he could turn and shoot with a little more accuracy.

He'd tear the bastard's throat out, but he had a gut feeling that a gun was pointed at his head right now.

He was a vampire, but bullets placed in the right body parts would definitely kill him.

And that really sucked.

Jacob gave a long stare at the shadows around the car, and that was when he saw the man's reflection in the back window. He studied the image for a moment and then spun, unloading the gun into the guy's body. A look of shock crossed the hunter's face right before he fell to the ground, blood instantly pooling around him. In the darkness, the blood looked black.

Jacob tugged the leash, pulling Mango away as he hurried in the direction of the manor. He wasn't going to stick around for the cops to show up. Explaining why he killed the man would be hard enough. Explaining his fangs would be impossible.

* * * *

Shelby took one look across the club at his mate and instantly knew something was wrong. It was a feeling, a rhythm of emotion that seemed to surround Jacob as he walked into the club. His shoulders were stiff, his strides angry.

Hurrying toward his mate, Shelby wondered what could have happened. Jacob was at the manor. Had something bad happened at home? The shifters were there, even if they weren't on the clock at night. And some of the coven was there as well. Not everyone came to The Manacle.

He caught Jacob's arm as his mate headed down the hallway to Christian's office. "What's wrong?"

Jacob turned and looked down at him. His shoulders were stiff and his body rigid. When his eyes landed on Shelby, he relaxed under Shelby's hand. But Shelby caught the look of pain, anger…relief? It was all of the above and none of the above. He just wasn't sure.

"Come with me." Jacob's voice was warm with anger as he grabbed Shelby's arm and walked toward Christian's office. Whatever was wrong, he would find out when Jacob told Christian.

Why did he have a feeling he wasn't going to like it?

Jacob knocked once and then entered, releasing Shelby to close the door.

"Problem?" Christo asked. Christian was nowhere in sight.

"The prince around?"

"No," Christo said as he stood from the meeting table. "I'm in charge when he is absent."

"I ran into a hunter tonight," Jacob said as he ran his hand over his short-cropped hair. "He was spouting off about letting the world know vampires existed and telling me about how his small group of hunters would be worldwide when everyone learned of our existence."

"What did you do?" Christo asked.

Shelby stood there shaking. That was the second time Jacob had run into a hunter. His stomach felt like a tight knot as he listened.

"I shot his ass."

Christo nodded. "Dead?"

"No, I just tickled him with the bullets," Jacob retorted.

Christo smiled. "So he acknowledged that the group was small?"

"Blabbered that part," Jacob answered. "Why do men who are about to kill feel the need to confess all?"

Christo chuckled this time. Shelby didn't find it funny in the least. It wasn't Christo's mate out there getting harassed by vampire hunters. Shelby had an urge to smack him.

"I'll let Christian know this tidbit of information."

Shelby grabbed Jacob's hand and practically pulled him from the office, rounding on his mate as soon as the door was closed. "You could have died, again," he pointed out angrily. "What is with you and death?"

It was a legitimate question. He just had a feeling he was asking the wrong person. Fate would have been the one to ask.

"I'm not looking for death, Shelby," Jacob answered, his stance and tone a little more relaxed than when he first walked into the club. "But I'm not going to hide at home or here, either."

Shelby knew that Jacob was right, even if he didn't like it. "Then I'll have to teach you how to disseminate."

"I was hoping you would." Jacob leaned closer, pinning Shelby against the wall. Did shooting someone turn the guy on? His eyes were liquid pools of lust as he gazed down at Shelby, and damn if Shelby wasn't putty in the man's hands when he looked at him like that.

Jacob winked at Shelby and then grabbed his hand, leading him through the club and then to one of the back rooms. Shelby wasn't too sure about this. He wasn't into the whole BDSM scene. Sure, he had spied in the rooms from time to time, but that was pure curiosity. Just because he was curious, didn't mean he wanted to try it.

"Jacob?" Shelby asked, his voice shaky.

"I just want some privacy, hon. Don't get nervous."

Shelby swallowed. He was nervous.

Jacob nodded at Vaughn, the bouncer for the BDSM rooms, and then walked into one of the rooms that had a door open. Shelby glanced around the room, remembering the last time he was brought in here.

"I promise, Shelby, just sex."

"You won't try and tie me down?" Shelby saw a flash of anger in Jacob's eyes as his jaw muscle tightened.

"No, I would never do anything to you that you didn't want, understand?"

Shelby nodded.

"But you can get naked for me." Jacob came up behind Shelby, wrapping his strong arms around Shelby's body. "And let me fuck you."

Shelby could do that. Heck, he was all for it. He glanced at the door and then began to undress. Shelby knew Vaughn wouldn't let anyone walk in on them. That was part of his job, to make sure no one busted in while others were using the room.

He felt a little awkward when Jacob leaned against one of the tables, crossing his arms over his chest and watching Shelby shed his clothing. "Aren't you going to get undressed?"

"In a minute. I'm enjoying the show."

Show? Shelby was just getting undressed. What kind of a show was that?

Kicking his shoes off, Shelby bent over and pushed his pants down to his ankles, hearing a low groan from behind him. He smiled. Wiggling his ass, Shelby removed his pants and set them on a table close to the door. "Show's over."

"No," Jacob said as he approached Shelby, his walk smooth, seductive, and as leisurely as a cat. "The show has only just begun."

Shelby's pounding heart began to buzz in his ears as Jacob drew closer, a wicked grin on his face. He lifted Shelby from his feet, laying him on his back across one of the tables. Shelby watched as Jacob sank to his knees and took Shelby's cock into his mouth.

Oh hell, he liked this show.

He placed his feet on Jacob's shoulders as his mate sucked his cock with expertise. Shelby was whimpering, moaning, keening, and begging by the time Jacob stood, a cocky smile on his lips.

Shelby panted as he lay there watching Jacob unfasten his pants. Oh, this was going to be quick and dirty. Shelby liked quick and dirty.

Grabbing a bottle of lube from the shelf, Jacob poured the gel onto his fingers and then slid them into Shelby's ass as he stroked his erection. Shelby was so turned on by the sight that he was ready to come.

When Jacob removed his fingers and pressed his cock into Shelby, he damn near shouted with joy. Shelby tilted his head to the side, ready to fall apart, ready to explode…he wasn't sure what was going on as his body shook and shivered, but he knew he wanted Jacob to bite him in his tender flesh and make him shout his release.

Jacob poised his head, his fangs sharp and white, and then he leaned forward, the tips breaking through Shelby's flesh, the feeling of utter bliss coursing through him as Jacob sank his teeth into Shelby. He drank from Shelby as he fucked him with speed only possessed by a true vampire.

"Jacob!" Shelby shouted as his seed painted their bodies. He felt Jacob pull his teeth away and lick the wound before he roared his release.

Hell, Shelby would gladly come back here anytime Jacob wanted to fuck him. It had been quick, and Shelby had damn near lost his mind.

That was good enough for him.

Jacob pulled free, helping Shelby to his shaky feet.

"Damn, baby," Jacob said as he leaned forward and kissed Shelby. "I needed that."

"Anytime," Shelby said exhaustedly as he waved a hand at Jacob. Jacob chuckled as he grabbed Shelby's pants and helped him slide into them. His legs were shaky as hell.

"Are you steady?" Jacob asked.

"Steady enough." He grinned.

Jacob cupped Shelby's face. His light-brown eyes looked like coppery satin as he smiled down at Shelby. "My little vampire."

Shelby grinned like a fool. "My Jacob."

"Are you ready to teach me how to pop from place to place?" Jacob asked as he opened the door, stepping aside so Shelby could pass.

"Are you ready to stop letting death find you?"

Jacob chuckled. "I thought you were the one who told me that this life was dangerous."

He had, but that didn't mean Shelby wouldn't worry about Jacob for the rest of eternity.

THE END

WWW.LYNNHAGEN.COM

ABOUT THE AUTHOR

Lynn Hagen loves writing about the somewhat flawed, but lovable. She also loves a hero who can see past all the rough edges to find the shining diamond of a beautiful heart.

You can find her on any given day curled up with her laptop and a cup of hot java, letting the next set of characters tell their story.

For all titles by Lynn Hagen, please visit
www.bookstrand.com/lynn-hagen

Siren Publishing, Inc.
www.SirenPublishing.com

Lightning Source UK Ltd.
Milton Keynes UK
UKOW031831100912

198792UK00016B/5/P

9 781622 413874